PUFFIN BOOKS

THE GROWING SUMMER

When Alex, Penny, Robin and Naomi went to stay with Great-Aunt Dymphna they all thought she was the most extraordinary person they had ever met.

'Could you tell us about meals and things?' they asked. 'What time is lunch?'

'When you're hungry of course. When else should it be?'

'But who cooks it?'

That clearly flummoxed Great Aunt Dymphna. 'Why you,' she said at last. 'Who else?'

From that moment they knew that this holiday with the aunt, more Irish than the Irish, who held conversations with the seagulls and lived in a lonely old house in a field miles from anywhere, would be utterly different from anything they had ever experienced.

Noel Streatfeild's father was a Church of England vicar, and she and her brother and sisters grew up in several vicarages in the south of England. More than most children's authors, she draws on exact memories of her own childhood for scenes in her own books, and her interest in stage children is a direct result of her own career in the theatre.

Other books by Noel Streatfeild

NOEL STREATFEILD

THE GROWING
SUMMER

Illustrated by
EDWARD ARDIZZONE

PUFFIN BOOKS
in association with Collins

PUFFIN BOOKS

Published by the Penguin Group
27 Wrights Lane, London W8 5TZ, England
Viking Penguin Inc., 40 West 23rd Street, New York, New York 10010, USA
Penguin Books Australia Ltd, Ringwood, Victoria, Australia
Penguin Books Canada Ltd, 2801 John Street, Markham, Ontario, Canada L3R 1B4
Penguin Books (NZ) Ltd, 182–190 Wairau Road, Auckland 10, New Zealand

Penguin Books Ltd, Registered Offices: Harmondsworth, Middlesex, England

First published by Collins 1966
Published in Puffin Books 1968
13 15 17 19 20 18 16 14

Copyright © Noel Streatfeild, 1966
All rights reserved

Made and printed in Great Britain by
BPCC Hazell Books Ltd
Member of BPCC Ltd
Aylesbury, Bucks, England
Set in Linotype Georgian

For
Elizabeth Enright

because I so greatly admire
her books

I am most grateful to Mrs Bambridge and A. P. Watt for permission to quote from Rudyard Kipling's 'Our Fathers of Old' and 'Cold Iron', both from *Rewards and Fairies*. Also to Miss D. E. Collins, Methuen and A. P. Watt for permission to quote from 'The Song of Quoodle' by G. K. Chesterton

Contents

1

Medway

THE Gareths lived in a suburb of London. The road where they lived was called Royal Crescent. All the houses in Royal Crescent were exactly alike in a style which the children's father called 'nineteenth-century shingle'. This meant the top half of each house had little stones stuck on it as if someone had thrown pebbles at it off some shingly beach. Each house had a name instead of a number, which was supposed to give distinction to the Crescent. The Gareths' house was called Medway. This name was not chosen by the Gareths but was the name the house had when they had moved in to it.

'Not much point in changing it,' the children's father had said. 'It's harmless and the postman knows it.'

'And it might have been worse,' the children's mother had pointed out, 'it might have been called Dun Roamin'.'

'Which,' the children's father had retorted, 'would have been particularly ill-chosen seeing we've never even started to roam.'

The Gareths also left their little front garden unaltered. This meant they had a lilac and a laburnum growing in it, which all the houses in the Crescent had unless the owners had dug them up and planted something grand like a magnolia. It had never crossed the children's father's mind to alter anything either in the house or in the garden for he had never had a belonging feeling. The children's mother came from New Zealand and when she became engaged her parents, who were on a visit to England, had found Medway and bought it, and had given it to their daughter and son-in-law as a wedding present. From his first sight of it the children's father had hated the house though he had never actually said so, and as the years passed he had got used to

it, in the way a person gets accustomed to having a limp.

'Silly old Daddy,' the children's mother would say when their father let something despising about Medway slip out, 'he loves it really, you should have seen his face when Grandfather and Grandmother first showed us the house.'

The children's father would smile inside when he heard that. Curious, he would think, how an expression of horror could be misread.

At first glance the Gareth family were very like the other families who lived in the Crescent, but they were not really for the children's father did work that was different from the other fathers. Most other fathers were junior chartered accountants, or solicitors, or they were in business, but the children's father was a kind of doctor. That is to say he had qualified as a doctor but his work was research. Outwardly he seemed like other people's fathers, mowing his little back lawn, washing his car or, in winter when there was snow, scraping it off the front path, but inside he was different. Nobody, not even the children, knew how different, for only part of him lived in Medway and even that part often wandered mentally back to the germs he was cultivating in the laboratory where he worked.

'Wake up, you old dreamer,' the children's mother would say. 'I don't believe you have been listening to a word I've been saying.'

If their father was different from the other fathers in the street the children fitted in like pips in an orange. Alex – short for Alexander – was thirteen going on fourteen. Penny – short for Penelope – was twelve. She and Alex went to the same school and were doing well in a non-spectacular way. Neither really liked games but you played them at school for the honour of The House, so they both tried hard and got into junior teams. Every day they came home looking like snails with all the homework on their backs. Every day as soon as tea was over they settled down to work without being told, for that was the only way they could keep their places in class. To lose their place in class both knew was the worst thing that could happen to anybody.

Robin and Naomi went to a junior school for Robin was ten and Naomi nine. The autumn after they were eleven they were to go to the same school as Alex and Penny, and it was expected they would do equally well.

All four children had chestnut-coloured hair and even that behaved properly. In other families where one member has curls it is often one of the boys who gets them, but in the Gareth family it was Naomi. Naomi, with her long dark eyelashes and curls, was an exceptionally pretty child, but this was never mentioned for fear of making her conceited. In any case the children's mother admired Penny more for she had what she thought was an interesting face, and her long straight hair suited her. Alex too was rather good-looking, but Robin was unlucky for he had a piece of hair that stood up on the crown of his head like a hollyhock in a bed of double daisies, which made him look like that sort of clown whose hair stands on end when he pulls a string.

It was an ordinary April afternoon when things that were not ordinary started to happen. The children were having tea and all trying to tell their mother something at the same time. Alex said:

'I'm being tried for the second junior cricket team on Saturday but I doubt I'll make it.'

Penny spread some jam on her bread.

'Oh, Mummy, I may be made an acting assistant librarian for the junior library, which would be a bit of luck because librarians get the pick of the new books.'

To Robin food was the most important thing you could talk about.

'Oh, Mummy, at school dinner we had the most awful pudding with bad dates in it.'

His mother cut the cake she had made. She knew the food at school, if unimaginative, was good for when her turn came round she helped to serve it, but it was understood all school food was uneatable so she did not argue.

'How terrible! Have some cake to take the taste away.'

Although her looks were never mentioned Naomi was nobody's fool; the world was full of looking-glasses so of course she knew she was pretty, and this made her dress-conscious.

'Mummy, this new summer frock is the teeniest bit too long.'

At the junior school the girls wore green check summer frocks. So far Naomi had worn the frocks Penny had worn in her last summer at the junior school but this term she had needed one new one. It was perfectly true it was longer than Penny's cast-offs, but it would probably fit Naomi by the end of the summer, but arguing would get the children's mother nowhere.

'All right, darling, when I get time I'll take up the hem.'

'Has Daddy heard from the caravan people?' Alex asked.

It was hard to winkle the children's father out of his laboratory, but unwillingly he agreed to a fortnight's holiday each year. For this he hired a caravan and the overflow slept in a tent. It was, the children's mother thought, a chancy kind of holiday, the English weather being what it was, and hard work for her because there was just as much cooking and shopping as usual only under more difficult

conditions. But other families in the Crescent went caravaning and they had talked about it so much that the children
had begged to be allowed to go caravaning, so each year
caravaning they went. This summer they were planning to
camp in Scotland.

'I don't know if Daddy's had the confirmation yet, they
don't send that until this month, we're down on the list all
right.' Then her head shot up. 'Listen! How extraordinary!
There's Daddy now.'

'Can't be,' said Alex, 'it's much too early.'

Naomi scrambled off her chair.

'It must be Daddy, nobody else has a key.'

John Gareth came into the hall, although he did not seem
to see her he gave Naomi a kiss.

'Where's Mummy?'

The children's mother came to the dining-room door.

'Here, darling. What's brought you home at ...?' Then
she stopped. 'What's happened?'

The children had joined their mother in the doorway so
they saw what prompted their mother's question. Something
had happened to their father since they had seen him at
breakfast. His face usually had a listening expression, like
people's faces when they are playing a piano or a violin, now
it had a shining look as if he could see something nobody
else could see. He caught hold of the children's mother.

'Come in the other room, Alice. I've got something to tell
you.'

The children wandered back to the table to finish their
tea.

'What's up, I wonder,' said Alex, 'it isn't like Daddy to
look so het up.'

Penny had moved into her mother's place.

'Anyone want any more tea? Perhaps he's found that
germ he's always looking for.'

Alex passed her his cup.

'It's not one germ, it's what makes an epidemic.'

Penny poured out the tea.

'Well, an epidemic of germs then.'

Robin cut himself another slice of cake.

'He might have won some money, that's just how Mr Pink at The Towers looked when he won that football pool.'

'You are silly!' said Naomi. 'You know Daddy doesn't do pools so how could he win?'

Alex got up.

'Perhaps he's got a rise, if he has he's sure to let us go to the Outer Isles when we're in Scotland. I'm going to start work – coming, Penny?'

As the door closed on Alex and Penny, Robin helped himself to jam and spread it on his slice of cake. This was not allowed, not because it was bad for Robin, but because his mother said she wasn't going to bake good cakes for him to mess up. Now he spoke with his mouth full, also not allowed.

'I think something extraordinary must have happened. Even on Christmas Eve Daddy doesn't come home early.'

'Not even on a birthday,' Naomi agreed, 'and most fathers get home for them.'

'Not even on the day before the summer holiday,' Robin added, 'though Mummy always asks him to try to.'

Naomi looked at the clock.

'And it isn't half past five and he never comes home before seven. Never.'

Robin looked regretfully at the remains of the cake.

'Pity, it isn't often I'm left alone with food and now that I am I've no room for more.'

Everything always happened in the same way in Medway. Tea over, the children's mother cleared the table at once so that Robin and Naomi could use it for their homework. Alex and Penny did their before supper homework in their bedrooms, but they did their after supper homework in the dining-room because by then Robin was going to bed in the boys' room and Naomi in the girls' room. Now it was after tea homework time and the table was not cleared.

'Do you think we better take the things to the kitchen?' Naomi suggested.

Robin fetched the tray from the sideboard.

'Let's. We'll put the plates and cups and tea things on this and we can carry the food out separately.'

Robin carried the loaded tray into the hall and Naomi came behind with the big teapot. Across the passage was the sitting-room and from it came the muffled sound of talking.

'Still at it,' said Robin. 'It's really most curious. Something must be up.'

It was as he said this that the words rang out from the sitting-room. It was their mother who was speaking, almost it was a scream.

'Leave the children for a year! It's impossible!'

2

The News

ROBIN and Naomi put the tray and the teapot in the kitchen.

'My goodness!' said Robin. 'What on earth was Mummy talking about? Leave us for a year!'

Naomi looked scared.

'Mothers and fathers don't leave children ever, not even for a little while.'

'I suppose it's Grandfather and Grandmother in New Zealand,' said Robin. 'They've always wanted us to go there.'

'But always all of us. They never thought Mummy would go without us.'

'She did say it was impossible,' Robin pointed out.

'But why should Daddy want to?'

'I don't know, it doesn't make sense. Come on, let's finish clearing the table.'

Naomi thought that a good idea.

'And we might hear some more, and it's not listening for we were only walking past.'

But they heard no more, only the low mutter of their father's voice with a sort of pleading sound in it.

On the cleared table the children spread out their books. Their homework only took an hour and after that there was television or reading out loud before supper and bed.

'It's to be hoped Mummy stops talking soon,' said Naomi, 'or we shan't be able to get in to watch television.'

'And I want to hear what's up. Such nonsense, leaving us for a year!'

But when at last the children's father and mother came out of the sitting-room no word was said to show what they had been talking about. The children's mother looked into the dining-room and saw the cleared table and Robin and Naomi at work.

'Oh, good children! Thank you for clearing for me.' Then she went away again and shut the door.

'Grown-ups!' Robin muttered. 'Fancy saying something like "leave the children for a year" and then nothing more. It's indecent.'

'She doesn't know we heard,' Naomi reminded him.

Robin was drawing a map of Australia. Suddenly he stopped.

'I vote we tell the others.'

'When?'

'Now. If that's what's happening they ought to know.'

Naomi was shocked. Hers and Robin's homework was not taken very seriously but the older ones' was, nobody ever interrupted it.

'We can't while they're working.'

Robin got up.

'I'm going to tell them if you're not. Imagine talk like that going on and them not knowing.'

Alex and Penny, though supposed to work in separate rooms, worked together when Penny needed help, which she always did when it was mathematics. It was mathematics that evening so she had joined Alex in the boys' bedroom. They both were bent over her exercise book when the door was quietly opened and Robin and Naomi came in.

Alex was furious.

'What on earth ...?' he started but Robin stopped him.

'Don't be cross. We thought you ought to know.'

'He means it's a family thing,' Naomi explained. 'I mean, imagine us left on our own!'

Penny stood up, all the colour fading from her cheeks. This had happened to other children, but never, never had she dreamed it could happen to them.

'You mean Mummy's leaving Daddy?'

Robin did not get on to what she was thinking.

'Of course not, whoever said she was? What we heard was ...'

'We weren't listening, truly we weren't,' Naomi put in. 'We were just clearing tea so we could do our homework and we had to pass the sitting-room door and ...'

Robin thought Naomi was telling the story too slowly.

'It was Mummy, she sort of cried out as if somebody had trodden on her toe, "Leave the children for a year! It's impossible!"'

Slowly Penny sank back to her chair.

'Leave us for a year,' she whispered. 'But why should they?'

'Whatever the reason I don't think they're telling us,' Robin said, 'for when Mummy came in she was just ordinary.'

Naomi shook her head.

'Not quite she wasn't. I was facing the door so I saw. She had been crying.'

Alex was startled. Mothers didn't cry.

'Are you sure?'

Naomi nodded.

'Absolutely. Sort of shiny on the cheeks and red round the eyes and at the end of her nose.'

What Robin and Naomi had heard was frightening but not so appalling as what for one silly moment she had imagined, so slowly colour was creeping back into Penny's cheeks.

'I expect they will tell us, after supper perhaps.'

Alex took control.

'You kids had better go back to the dining-room. Whatever's up we've got to get our homework done.'

'Will we say anything if they don't tell us?' Robin asked.

Alex was doubtful.

'I'm not sure. Get along now, I'll think what we ought to do and tell you before supper.'

Alone Penny and Alex stared at each other.

'They couldn't have heard wrong, could they?' Alex wondered.

Penny doodled on her exercise book.

'It didn't sound like it. But perhaps it isn't as bad as it sounds.'

Alex thought that an idiotic remark.

'How couldn't it be as bad as it sounds?'

Penny stabbed at her doodle.

'I suppose it couldn't. But whatever it is they must tell us.'

'Perhaps they won't because it's not happening,' Alex suggested. 'I mean, she did say "I simply can't".'

Penny thought about that.

'I think we'll have to tell them what Robin and Naomi heard. I mean it's no good us all stewing and worrying over it – especially if it's never going to happen.'

'Too true,' Alex agreed, 'we'd be listening and watching. If nothing's said by the end of supper I vote we come right out with it.'

'And if they don't want to tell us?'

'They're unlucky. I mean Robin and Naomi hearing. They couldn't expect we'd go on as usual – well, look at us now, fat lot of homework we've done.'

Penny picked up her pen, preparing to concentrate on mathematics.

'Will you tell them what the others heard?'

Alex dismissed that.

'Not much chance, it's Robin and Naomi's story. I don't see them letting me get away with their thunder.'

As far as the children's parents were concerned supper was meant to be an ordinary meal on an ordinary day. It was not, of course, for even if Robin and Naomi had not heard what they had heard, they would have felt something was in the air. First of all their mother was trying so desperately hard to make things ordinary, which made them un-ordinary straight away for she never behaved like that. Then their father, who never seemed to notice things like what someone else was eating, kept begging their mother to eat something, which she obviously did not want to do. It was all embarrassing and sort of sad somehow, and suddenly Alex couldn't bear it any more.

'I say, I think we ought to tell you something Robin and...'

Naomi, who was sitting next to her father, patted his hand.

'We weren't listening, truly we weren't.'

'It was us that heard so I'll tell,' said Robin. 'It was when we were clearing tea and we had to pass the sitting-room and we heard you, Mummy, sort of call out "Leave the children for a year! It's impossible!"'

Robin, without knowing it, had imitated the way his mother had sounded and the words rang through the dining-room like a seagull crying. There was a pause before anyone said anything more, then Penny spoke almost in a whisper.

'You aren't leaving us, Mummy, are you?'

It was her father who answered.

'I'm glad you told us what you heard, but if you' – he looked at Robin and Naomi – 'had told me right away it would have saved a lot of heart-burning. There's no thought of your mother leaving you. It's I who am going away.'

Penny's fears came sweeping back. This was how it started when parents separated. Girls it had happened to had told her so.

'But why, Daddy?'

Her father smiled at her.

'Don't look like that, Penny. It's only for a year, it will soon pass. Now I'll make this as simple as possible. You all know roughly about my work. Well, for quite a time now I've been trying to isolate a microbe, which is a killer when it gets going.'

'It's what starts a type of epidemic, isn't it?' Alex asked.

'That's what I believe but so far it's only theoretical. We have had no epidemic of this type in this country for centuries but there are outbreaks in other countries, notably in the Far East.'

In a flash of understanding Penny knew what was coming.

'So you want to go to the Far East?'

Her father looked at her gratefully.

'That's hit the nail on the head. But it's been a dream, I never thought it could happen. Then today I was offered a year's research, it's a roving commission, I can go anywhere where it looks as though an epidemic might blow up.'

Alex remembered the seagull sound in Robin's voice when he had imitated his mother.

'He must go, Mummy, you do see that.'

The children's mother had that sort of shine in her eyes that comes when tears are not far away.

'Of course I see it. It's a wonderful opportunity and of course he must take it. It's only the news came as a bit of a shock, but I'm getting used to it now.'

'When do you have to go?' Robin asked his father.

'In a couple of weeks.'

There were whistles and exclamations from all the children.

'What a rush!'

Their father nodded, trying to look serious, but they could see that the thought of dashing around buying tropical kit excited him, anyway he always hated talk that went on too long. He was a quiet sort of man. He got up.

'If you've all finished, your mother and I have a lot to do.'

3

Good-bye

S o in two weeks the children's father was gone. Until he was gone there was so much to do with shopping and packing, and Father not able to do much because of his inoculations, that the children's mother had no time to think how terribly she was going to miss him. Then one morning the taxi was at the door – he would not be seen off – his luggage was put into it, he gave a wave, then off he drove to London airport.

Father had known how that moment would feel for Mother.

'It's better for me,' he told the children, 'it's always easier for the traveller, it's the ones who stay at home who take the knock. That's why I've insisted on leaving on a Saturday.' He gave Alex an envelope. 'Here are tickets for a matinée. It won't be a cure but it will be a help. I rely on you children to do what you can to look after your mother and to cheer her up.'

So as soon as the taxi was round the corner Alex told his mother about the matinée and she said exactly what he hoped she would say.

'Oh, I couldn't go, darling, there's such a lot of clearing up to do here. You should see the mess your father's left.'

Of course the answer to that was that the children helped and soon the house was tidy, the shopping done, lunch eaten and the whole family were off to see a thrilling play with two murders in it.

Returning home everybody's spirits dropped as they turned into Royal Crescent. Medway looked so depleted with Father away. The children meant to cheer their mother up but something – the play perhaps – seemed to have done that for it was she who cheered them.

'I shall make the most enormous omelette and we'll have high tea, it will save two washings up. Then we'll play a game.'

It was after Robin and Naomi had gone to bed that their mother talked. She, Alex and Penny were having hot chocolate and biscuits round the fire when she started.

'I suppose you think this journey to the Far East was something unexpected that turned up, but it's not really, your father's been hankering to be off ever since we married.'

Alex and Penny were surprised. Their father had always seemed almost glued to his laboratory.

'He never said anything,' said Alex.

'You don't when something you want to do you know you never can do, in a way it was Grandfather and Grandmother's fault.'

Penny nearly choked over her chocolate. About every two years Grandfather and Grandmother came over from New Zealand for a visit. They did not stay in the house, there was no room, but in a hotel. They were darlings and seemed on the best of terms with their father.

'Daddy never seems to bear them a grudge.'

Her mother smiled.

'Oh, he doesn't. It was much more subtle than that. As you know, I'm the only girl in a family of four boys, so I wasn't popular when I insisted on coming to England to train as a nurse.'

'You wouldn't have met Daddy in hospital if you hadn't,' Penny reminded her.

'Of course I wouldn't. But meeting Daddy, or someone like him, was exactly what the grandparents were afraid I would do. For naturally they didn't want their only daughter living the other side of the world.'

'Can't blame them,' said Alex.

'No, I wouldn't be pleased if any of you wanted to live in New Zealand. But if I had to marry an Englishman they wanted me in one place where they could get hold of me, and that was not what your father and I had in mind. We had

planned to work for two years in a hospital in an unde-
veloped country.'

Alex helped himself to a biscuit.

'Goodness! I never knew that.'

'Nobody knew except us, though I think Grandfather and
Grandmother guessed it might happen.' Mother looked in
the fire, half smiling as if what she saw there amused her.
'Your grandfather and grandmother scotched it. They were
over here for the wedding and one day, without a hint of
what they were up to, bought this house. They gave it to us
as a wedding present.'

Penny thought lovingly of the house.

'Weren't you pleased?'

Her mother nodded.

'I suppose I was, every woman wants a home, but I don't
think your father would have settled down without a fight,
only the right job for him turned up. That, and because we
had a house, turned the scales.'

Alex took a sip of his chocolate.

'And then I was born.'

'Yes. So then we were well and truly anchored.'

'But Daddy's never given up the idea of working abroad?'

'Now, wait a minute, Alex, that's not quite right. He's
been trying to isolate an almost invisible microbe which, if
he's right, could be the cause of a terrible disease. If he could
find that microbe in the blood of people suffering from the
disease I don't know if it would be proof – but it would take
the world a step nearer finding a cure.'

'You mean he might be famous?' Penny asked.

'Some day, I suppose. Yes. He's a brilliant man, your
father.'

Penny nodded. Of course they all knew Father had a
brain.

'Do you suppose Daddy hated the house at first, like he
still sometimes says he does?'

'He might have thought he did but I'm sure he doesn't
now. Anyway it's been good for him having a home for
remember he never had one after he was twelve.'

Father's mother and father had been killed by a bomb in 1940. A part of the family history to which the children were attached, for it was dramatic that no other children they knew had a grandfather and a grandmother who had been killed by a bomb.

'Poor Daddy,' said Penny. 'It must have been awful for him when the headmaster told him what had happened. Imagine having no relations when you were only twelve.'

'Well, he had that aunt,' her mother reminded her.

Father's Aunt Dymphna, who lived in Ireland, was to the children more like a character in a book than a real person. At the time when his parents were killed their father had been at a boarding school in the west country. He had spent his Christmas and Easter holidays at school for the headmaster had a boy about his age, but for the summer holidays he had been sent to Ireland to stay with his Aunt Dymphna.

Aunt Dymphna, so the legend went, before the war had run some kind of small school in France. When war was declared she had escaped in a coal boat carrying all she could save of her worldly goods in a canvas hold-all. The boat had docked in England but Aunt Dymphna had not stayed there but had departed immediately for the Republic of Ireland. There she had bought a very ramshackle old house in West Cork, which had once been someone's stately home; it was called Reenmore.

The children's father had never said much about those holidays in Ireland but the children had always felt, from the little he did say, that there was something queer about them. Once when the children had 'flu he had remarked:

'Your great-aunt Dymphna would have a fit if she could see all these pills and bottles of medicine; she never believed in any cure unless she had picked it and made it up herself.'

Once when the school uniform was being discussed he had said:

'I wonder where my school clothes came from? I suppose the lawyer ordered them or told the school to, certainly it wasn't Aunt Dymphna who bought them. I dread to think what I would have worn if she'd had a hand in it.'

On the first caravan holiday, when their father had shown himself unexpectedly efficient about building a picnic fire, he had explained his proficiency by saying:

'I learnt to cook my own food when I stayed with Aunt Dymphna. Come to that I had to snare or catch most of what I ate for she was often away for days together. You soon learn to look after yourself when you are hungry.'

Alex, remembering these things when his mother said, 'Well, he had that aunt,' burst out:

'I reckon old Great-Aunt Dymphna is raving mad.'

His mother pounced on that.

'Not a bit of it. Actually she must be a most remarkable woman. Daddy respected her even when he was a boy, and he certainly does now.'

'He never goes to see her,' Penny pointed out, 'though she only lives in Ireland, which isn't far.'

'That's true. But I think it's because he doesn't want to make work for her for she lives quite alone, as far as I can gather, in an enormous house.'

'Funny to be Daddy and have so few relations,' said Penny. 'Look what a lot we've got. An uncle in South Africa and three in New Zealand and rows of cousins, and a grand-father and a grandmother and all of us.'

Alex poured himself out some more chocolate.

'It was unlucky for Daddy he hadn't any grandparents. Most children have them, don't they, Mummy?'

'There was a grandmother on one side and a grandfather on the other at the time Daddy's parents were killed, but they lived alone and couldn't cope with a boy of twelve. They're both dead now, as you know. Yes, he had remark-ably few relations.'

Penny was sitting next to her mother on the sofa, now she snuggled up to her.

'Perhaps it's us that are very lucky. I just couldn't imagine having no relations. Poor Daddy, it must have been awful.'

Her mother put an arm round her.

'You wait till that promised visit to New Zealand comes off. Perhaps then you'll think you have too many relations.' Alex helped himself to another biscuit.

'I suppose our going is further off than ever now – I mean Daddy won't get away again for ages, will he?'

His mother held out her hand for a biscuit.

'We couldn't have gone this year anyway even if we could afford it, because as you know, Grandfather and Grandmother are in South Africa visiting your uncle there and his family, then next year, all being well, they'll come and visit us.'

'Perhaps the year after,' said Penny.

Her mother smiled. Going to New Zealand was, as far as she could see, only a castle in the air and likely to stay that way.

'Perhaps the year after,' she agreed. 'We'll see. But I want to tell you both about something much nearer. This year's holiday. Will you mind very much if I cancel that caravan?'

Both Alex and Penny tried not to sound as if they minded but they did. Caravaning was a high spot of the year. Their mother might just as well have said 'Will you mind if we miss out Christmas?'

'Why do you want to?' Penny asked.

'I don't think I could cope alone. I know you'll all help but it's when things go wrong, like the water not being delivered or the man who owns the site not doing something he's promised to do ...'

'That doesn't often happen,' said Alex.

'Often enough. What I planned instead, if you agree, was to go to a small hotel near a loch – you know, where there's fishing and boating and things like that. It would be a wonderful holiday for me, no shopping, no cooking, no washing up.'

Penny looked reproachful.

'You know we nearly always help wash up.'

Her mother could have answered, 'You do indeed when you are there, but you are always dashing off somewhere with your father,' but she bit that back and instead said:

'You've no idea what a treat it is not to think "What shall we eat today?"'

Alex liked the sound of a hotel near a loch with a boat and fishing – who would not? – but his father had said he relied on them all to do what they could to look after Mother. Presumably, with Father away, she had to take care of the money. It would be a poor way of looking after her to let her spend more than they could afford on the holiday.

'Won't a hotel be expensive?'

Mother gave him a look as if to say what a help it was to have a thoughtful son.

'It's all right. Daddy found out about hotels before he left. There's not a lot of difference in the cost, it's up to you children to decide which we shall do.'

'Then of course it's the hotel,' said Alex. 'I didn't know you didn't like a caravan.'

'Anyway,' Penny added, 'we'd all like a hotel, it will be fun.'

Mother looked at the clock.

'I'm glad that's settled. I'll write off and book tomorrow. Do you think Robin and Naomi will agree?'

Alex did not say so but he knew Robin and Naomi would agree or he would have something to say to them.

'Of course.'

Mother got up.

'It's bedtime. Isn't it extraordinary to think that your father is at this moment over somewhere like Arabia? I'll tell you a secret: his first idea was that I should go with him. Imagine my deserting you children!'

Penny said:

'If there weren't any of us would you have liked to go?'

Her mother hugged her to her.

'I don't know because I can't imagine there being no you. I suppose it would be exciting to travel. I can't picture being over Arabia, can you?'

Arabia! It was mostly desert on a map. A drawing with no life to it, and somewhere above it was their father. The room that had seemed so cosy a minute ago was now chilly and full of shadows. Quickly Alex and Penny kissed their mother good night and hurried up to bed.

4

Packing Up

You can get used to anything, even to your father being away. In no time life in Medway was nearly back to normal. Sometimes the routine was broken by letters from Father full of wonderful descriptions of houses built on stilts, temples with golden roofs and tinkling bells, hyenas, snakes and tarantulas. To Mother he wrote more serious letters about his work, and parts of these letters she read to the children. But he was always moving and as he moved he was farther away from post offices, so letters came at longer and longer intervals. Meanwhile all the ordinary things filled the children's lives. School things and parties on Saturdays and Sundays – all the ordinary summer excitements.

Then one day a telegram came. It was not sent to the children's mother but to the hospital where their father worked. Someone came round from the hospital to see her. Their father was desperately ill, it was advised that their mother should fly out immediately.

The children were in school when the message arrived; by the time Alex and Penny got home from school everything was settled. Mother was looking pale but she was calm.

'Daddy's ill, I'm flying out to him first thing in the morning. My plane goes to Bangkok and I can get on to where Father is from there.' She looked at Alex. 'I'll have to leave you in charge. I've managed to get in touch with your Great-Aunt Dymphna, she is expecting you tomorrow. Seats have been booked in the afternoon for you on the aeroplane to Cork. A car will meet you there and take you to Reenmore!'

It was all too shattering to take in at once. Silly, unimportant things sprang to their minds. Penny looked at her satchel of homework.

'Have you told our schools?'

Mother had somehow thought of everything.

'Of course. I sent a note to both. The neighbours have been wonderful. Mr Jones at The Cedars is something to do with a travel agency. He's booked your seats and is arranging for someone to take you to the airport. The hospital have been wonderful too, they've booked my flight.'

'Are you packed?' Penny asked.

'Oh, yes – it's your packing we have to think about now. It will mean paying overweight but you'll have to take most of your clothes. I gather it's often chilly in Ireland even in summer. Besides, we don't know how long you'll have to stay.'

It was as their mother said this that the full awfulness of what was happening hit Alex and Penny and, in a lesser degree, Robin and Naomi.

'Is Daddy very ill?' Penny asked, trying not to let her voice wobble.

'Of course he is, idiot,' said Alex, who was cross because he was scared. 'You don't suppose Mummy would be going otherwise.'

Their mother managed to keep to herself how very small the chance was that their father would live.

'I'm afraid it may be some weeks before he's convalescent. When he is I hope I shall persuade him to fly home.'

Robin voiced what they were all thinking.

'Why must we go to Great-Aunt Dymphna? Why can't we stay here until you come back?'

'Yes, couldn't we?' Naomi pleaded. 'You see, we don't know Great-Aunt Dymphna and we do everybody here.'

Mother saw she would have to explain.

'I'm sure you'd manage very well, but school is a full-time job; when would you shop and cook and do the housework?'

'People would help,' Penny suggested. 'I know they would.'

'I know they would too,' their mother agreed. 'But you're not old enough to be left on your own. I'm not sure you'd be allowed to be by law. Imagine if the law said you'd all got to go to a home.'

'Isn't there somebody who could sleep here?' Alex suggested.

His mother looked at him.

'Tell me who? Of course it was the first thing I thought of.'

Who? The children racked their brains. There was a Mrs Sims who came and helped at spring-cleaning and times like that. But she had a husband and home and children to look after.

'Can't you get people from agencies?' Penny suggested.

'Certainly you can, or perhaps I might have got somebody through one of the schools, perhaps a teacher would have helped out, but arranging a thing like that takes time, and that I haven't got. I had to send a telegram to your Great-Aunt Dymphna for she is not on the telephone, but she got to a telephone to answer me; luckily I knew by then what time your plane would arrive.'

'Are you going to lock this house up?' Alex asked.

'Like we do on a holiday. I shall give the keys to the Maples next door. They'll look in every day just as I do for them when they're away.'

'I suppose Scotland's off,' said Alex. 'Have you told the hotel?'

'Yes. I sent them a telegram.'

'Will we do lessons at Great-Aunt Dymphna's?' Robin asked.

'I must leave that to her,' his mother explained. 'But as it's July and it will soon be holidays I should think not. I don't expect it will be worth you starting in a new school for a few weeks.' She could see more questions were coming which she could not answer, so she pointed up the stairs. 'Now you really must come up so that we can get on with your packing. If you'll all lay on your beds the clothes you suggest you should take I can see if anything's been overlooked.'

It was late before the last suitcase was packed. As nobody knew anything about Great-Aunt Dymphna's house they took clothes for every occasion: ordinary clothes, best clothes for parties, bathing things, wet weather clothes, fine weather clothes. It was an awful lot of luggage.

'If there is bathing,' their mother said, 'you are in charge, Alex. You others are to obey him as you would me when you are in the water.' With so many clothes to pack there was very little room for games and books. 'I'm sorry, darlings,' she apologized as she put the books and games back on the shelves, 'but you're terribly overweight already, and you can buy anything you want when you get there.'

When all the packing and labelling was done the children got into their pyjamas and dressing-gowns and came down for a picnic supper. Their favourite supper was a fry up of leftovers which Penny, when she was tiny, had christened a m-over, which was the nearest she could get to leftovers. Mother cooked a glorious m-over that night. It was eggs and sausages and meat and tomatoes and mushrooms, but in spite of its being so good no one was very hungry.

'Don't worry,' Mother said when they were washing up. 'You'll be able to have a big lunch tomorrow. I've arranged with Mr Jones, The Cedars, that you have it at the airport. I believe it's a lovely restaurant and you can watch all the planes arriving and taking off.'

Penny took Robin and Naomi up to bed after that. Luckily they were so tired it looked as if they would go to sleep right away, which was fortunate for them for there was a terrible lot nobody wanted to think about.

There was even more that Mother did not want to think about, but she was determined to keep emotion at arms' length. Alone with Alex she sounded really businesslike. She took an envelope out of her desk.

'There is twenty-five pounds in here. I needn't tell you to look after it. You'll have to pay for overweight luggage and I want you to send a cable to the address enclosed telling me you have arrived safely. You can send a delayed cable, which means you can send more words for less money. The post office will explain. Also in the envelope is a cheque for another twenty-five pounds. If you need that for anything you must ask your Great-Aunt Dymphna to cash it for you.'

'What am I likely to want all that money for?'

'Oh, one never knows and I shouldn't like you to be short. See the children behave well, won't you? You must give them their pocket money every week. I shall tell Robin and Naomi they must take orders from you – after your great-aunt of course – but you may have to act the elder brother occasionally. Penny will back you up.'

Alex, feeling awful, put the envelope in his pocket.

'What about letters?'

'I shall try and write but the first you will hear from me will be a cable telling you I've arrived and how Daddy is. I'll find out how long letters are likely to take, but we may have to stick to cables.' She broke off there and they gazed miserably at each other. Then she added briskly: 'We mustn't be silly, Alex, it's all hateful of course. But fix your mind on my coming home with Daddy – it's the only way to look at it.'

Penny came down then.

'They're ready for tucking up – and I think I'll go to bed too.'

'Sensible girl! Will you lock up, Alex? It's time we were all in bed. I've got an early start.'

Climbing the stairs Penny said:

'Will you send us a cable – about Daddy I mean?'

'Of course, lots I expect. I've just been telling Alex I will and you are sending some to me. I should think we may have to communicate mostly by letter telegrams. It will make us feel nice and close knowing the message was only sent off a few hours before we get it.'

Outside the girls' room her mother gave Penny a quick hug.

'I'll say good night to you here. I am leaving you and Alex in charge and I know you'll manage splendidly.' She saw Penny was not far from tears so she gave her a little pat. 'Hurry into bed, darling. You've a long day tomorrow.'

Penny did hurry into bed because she did not want her mother or Alex to see her face. In bed she pulled the bed-clothes over her head and cried and cried.

'It's a good thing to get this over,' she told herself between sobs, 'because after Mummy's gone I certainly mustn't cry, it'll be my job to cheer the little ones up. But, oh dear, how simply awful it all is. Daddy's going to die. I feel it in my bones he is.'

5

The Journey

THE children's mother left early the next morning. Her going was mercifully quick, and somehow nobody cried though Naomi was very near it. Luckily there was so much to do there was no time to think after she was gone, for it had been left to the children to close the house.

There are people who go away who just shut the front door, not bothering about the house, but the children's mother was not like that. Even with all the rush of the day before she had found time to cancel the newspapers and the milk, but she had to leave the actual covering up and locking up to the children. Alex, who was very conscious of the twenty-five pounds in money and the cheque in his pocket, feeling like the leader of an important expedition, gave his orders.

'Penny and Naomi, you do upstairs, Robin and I will do downstairs.'

'Don't you think,' Penny suggested, 'it would be better if we put the last things in our cases first and then put the luggage in the hall? It will be in the way when we are clearing the bedrooms.'

Alex knew he ought to have thought of that himself, so he was annoyed that he hadn't.

'All right,' he said ungraciously. 'I don't mind.'

'I hope Alex isn't going to be cross,' Naomi whispered to Penny.

'I'm sure he won't,' Penny comforted her. 'It's just he's fussed. Give me your washing things and your brush and comb and I'll pack them.'

Closing the house upstairs was quite a job. All the beds had to be stripped and the sheets and pillow cases put in the laundry basket. Then every bit of furniture had to be

covered in dust sheets, and small things wrapped in newspaper and all cupboards and drawers locked. But at last
Penny called down the stairs:

'We've finished up here, Alex. Will you two fetch the
laundry basket, it's to go in the next-door garage. The
laundry man knows about it.'

'Come on, Robin,' Alex muttered. 'You'd think to hear
the way Penny's going on that we didn't know where the
laundry goes.'

'Girls!' Robin said. 'They always flap, pay no attention.'

All four then inspected the house and agreed it had never
been more closed up, even when their mother was in charge.
Naomi gave a big sniff.

'Lucky Mrs Maple is coming in to open the windows sometimes, already it's got a gone-away smell.'

'Look at the time!' said Alex. 'It's after eleven and we're
being fetched at half past. Go on, everybody, get ready.'

A cheerful-looking young man came to fetch them in a car.

'All fixed?' he asked. 'Name of George, I'm Mr Jones's nephew.'

'Everything's done,' said Alex, 'except when we've got the luggage out I have to lock up and take the key next-door.'

The young man picked up two of the cases.

'O.K.,' he said. 'You two girls get in the car. I don't know about you but already I'm peckish for that lunch at the air-port.'

The children had not only never travelled alone before but when they travelled it had always been by car, so they expected the journey to Ireland to be a great adventure. But of course it was not. George was a wonderful man. He found out what each of them liked most to eat, which was chicken Maryland, and then was so knowledgeable about aeroplanes, which kept arriving and taking off, that without thinking the children ate everything on their plates and agreed ice-cream and fruit salad would be a perfect pudding. When it was time to go on board he knew exactly where they had to go and stayed with them until they had to go through to the departure lounge, where non-travellers were not allowed. Even there the children had no time to think for almost at once their flight was called and they were following the other passengers to the bus which took them to the aero-plane.

It was clear all the other passengers were used to travelling on aeroplanes, for they got into their seats and fastened their seat belts as if they did it every day. One boy, who was wear-ing dark glasses and looked as if he was only about eleven and who seemed to be travelling alone, not only strapped himself in as if he did it every day but at once opened a comic and began to read it. So it was a great humiliation to the children when the stewardess had to help them with their seat belts. The boy travelling alone was sitting just in front of Alex and Penny, and Alex was certain he was laughing at them.

'I bet he didn't know how to do it the first time,' he whispered to Penny, gesturing towards the boy.

'I noticed him in the lounge,' Penny whispered back. 'So odd to wear those black glasses all the time, even indoors.'

'Bad eyes, I suppose,' Alex muttered, and forgot about the strange boy.

The flight between London and Cork is very short and the children seemed scarcely to have finished the tea the stewardess brought them when they were told to fasten their seat belts again as they were landing. It was only then that Alex and Penny began to feel anxious. Penny said:

'I think we ought to do something about Robin and Naomi before they see Great-Aunt Dymphna, they've got awfully dirty since we started this morning.'

Alex nodded.

'Come to that we don't look too spruce ourselves, but I think there'll be time at the airport, George said we might have to wait quite a bit for our luggage coming off the plane.'

At the airport the children discovered they would have had time to have had baths if there had been any. There they sat, washed and brushed with their luggage round them, and nobody came to claim them.

'It's not possible to miss us,' Alex said to Penny. 'I mean, whoever's coming must have been told to pick up two boys and two girls and no grown-ups, and we're the only ones.'

Penny looked round the reception hall. It was true, of the passengers who had flown with them only four were left: one man talking to a friend, two nuns quietly reading and the boy in the black glasses, who was sitting close to them and who was still buried in his comic.

'They all look as if they were expecting to wait. It's only us who look worried,' Robin said in what he considered a whisper but which was pretty penetrating all the same. 'That boy was sick in a paper bag, me and Naomi watched him. He thought nobody saw.'

Naomi leant forward.

'And the stewardess brought him soda water to drink.'
Robin's whisper grew more piercing.

'Not out loud but inside we laughed and laughed, him being sick after looking so proud and none of us was.'

'Shut up, you two,' Alex said fiercely, 'he can hear what you say.'

But if the boy could hear there was no sign he had for with an unmoved face he went on reading.

Alex looked for the twentieth time at his watch.

'Whoever's meeting us might have sent a message if they were going to be late, but there was nothing for us on that message board, I looked.'

Penny saw that Naomi was frightened, so she managed to sound calm though she did not feel it.

'You know Great-Aunt Dymphna hasn't a telephone at Reenmore so how could she send a message?'

'And perhaps the roads are crowded,' Alex suggested, though he did not believe it.

Penny again tried to help.

'Mummy said Great-Aunt Dymphna telephoned from Bantry, which she said was twelve miles away. She said she telephoned from there because she could shop at the same time.'

Robin looked horrified.

'Twelve miles to a shop! What happens when we want ice-cream or something like that?'

'I bet there'll be a shop nearer for those sort of things,' said Alex. 'I expect Great-Aunt Dymphna goes to Bantry sort of once a week for the big shopping, you know, like Mummy goes on Fridays to get everything for the week-end.'

The stewardess off their plane passed through the hall. She saw the children and the boy in black glasses, she stopped by him first. Evidently something had interested him in his comic for he had taken out a pencil and was writing on the margin of it.

'Is somebody meeting you?' the stewardess asked. They could not hear what the boy answered but evidently it satisfied the stewardess. 'Good,' she said. 'Lots of people combine shopping in Cork with picking passengers up here.'

The stewardess then came up to the children.

'Who's collecting you four?'

'A car,' Alex explained. 'We are going to stay with an aunt ...'

'A great-aunt really,' Robin interrupted.

Alex frowned at him to keep quiet.

'She lives at a house called Reenmore in West Cork.'

'We think that perhaps she's held up by traffic,' said Penny.

The stewardess smiled.

'She might be if there's a fair anywhere, that is what we call a market in this country, but I dare say it's just that you aren't used to Ireland yet, time doesn't mean as much here as it does in England.'

'Anyway she can't send a message if the car is going to be late,' said Robin. 'Her nearest place to telephone is twelve miles away, it's called Bantry.'

Alex was going to say that Robin was talking rubbish, there was probably a telephone much nearer, but the stewardess spoke first.

'I wish I could wait with you but we're just off to London. Have a lovely time in West Cork, it's a glorious part of the country.'

The children looked after the stewardess as if they were saying good-bye to their last friend in the world. The boy in the dark glasses looked after her too. Then, when she was out of sight, he got up and walked out of the airport. The children were surprised.

'But nobody who is shopping in Cork called for him,' said Robin.

'I suppose he just got tired of sitting,' Penny suggested. 'I know I am.'

Robin was getting cross.

'And me.'

Naomi was obviously near tears, which did not surprise Alex, who was feeling pretty low himself.

'How about something to eat?' he suggested.

Penny shook her head.

'I couldn't eat a thing, and anyway we ought to wait here so that whoever comes for us sees us.'

Naomi, who was terribly tired, suddenly could bear waiting no longer. She burst into loud hiccupping sobs.

'Nobody is coming for us. Never. I want Mummy. I want to go home.'

'Tiffs and tantrums, what is happening here? Want Mummy. Want home. What next?'

The children jumped. There in front of them stood the most extraordinary old woman they had ever seen. Penny kept her head. She stood up and said politely her own version of something she had learnt that someone had said to Livingstone:

'Great-Aunt Dymphna I presume.'

6

Reenmore

THE first impression of Great-Aunt Dymphna was that she was more like an enormous bird than a great-aunt. This was partly because she wore a black cape, which seemed to flap behind her when she moved. Then her nose stuck out of her thin wrinkled old face just like a very hooked beak, On her head she wore a man's tweed hat beneath which straggled wispy white hair. She wore under the cape a shapeless long black dress. On her feet, in spite of it being a fine warm evening, were rubber boots.

The children gazed at their great-aunt, so startled by her appearance that the polite greetings they would have made vanished from their minds. Naomi was so scared that, though tears went on rolling down her cheeks, she did not make any more noise. Great-Aunt Dymphna had turned her attention to the luggage.

'Clutter, clutter! I could never abide clutter. What have you got in all this?' As she said 'this' a rubber boot kicked at the nearest suitcase.

'Clothes mostly,' said Alex.

'Mummy didn't know what we'd need,' Penny explained, 'so she said we'd have to bring everything.'

'Well, as it's here we must take it home I suppose,' said Great-Aunt Dymphna. 'Bring it to the car,' and she turned and, like a great black eagle, swept out.

Both at London airport and when they had arrived at Cork a porter had helped with the luggage. But now there was no porter in sight and it was clear Great-Aunt Dymphna did not expect that one would be used. Alex took charge.

'You and Naomi carry those two small cases,' he said to Robin. 'If you could manage one of the big ones, Penny, I can take both mine and then I'll come back for the rest.'

Afterwards the children could never remember much about the drive to Reenmore. Great-Aunt Dymphna, in a terrifyingly erratic way, drove the car. It was a large incredibly old black Austin. As the children lurched and bounced along – Robin in front, the other three in the back – Great-Aunt Dymphna shot out information about what they met in passing.

'Never trust cows when there's a human with them. Plenty of sense when on their own. Nearly hit that one but only because that stupid man directed the poor beast the wrong way.'

As they flashed past farms dogs ran out barking, prepared at risk of their lives to run beside the car.

'Never alter course for a dog,' Great-Aunt Dymphna shouted, 'just tell him where you are going. It's all he wants.' Then, to the dog: 'We are going to Reenmore, dear.' Her system worked for at once the dog stopped barking and quietly ran back home.

For other cars or for bicycles she had no respect at all.

'Road hogs,' she roared. 'Road hogs. Get out of my way or be smashed, that's my rule.'

'Oh, Penny,' Naomi whispered, clinging to her. 'We'll be killed, I know we will.'

Penny was sure Naomi was right but she managed to sound brave.

'I expect it's all right. She's been driving all her life and she's still alive.'

The only road-users Great-Aunt Dymphna respected were what the children would have called gipsies, but which she called tinkers. They passed a cavalcade of these travelling, not in the gipsy caravans they had seen in England, but in a different type with rounded tops. Behind and in front of the caravans horses ran loose.

'Splendid people tinkers,' Great-Aunt Dymphna shouted. Then, slowing down, she called out something to the tinkers which might, for all the children understood, have been in a foreign language. Then, to the children: 'If you need medicine they'll tell you where it grows.'

Alex took advantage of the car slowing down to mention the cable.

'We promised Mummy we'd send it,' he explained. 'And she's sending one to us to say she's arrived and how Daddy is.'

'Perhaps a creamery lorry will deliver it sometime,' Great-Aunt Dymphna said. 'That's the only way a telegram reaches me. You can send yours from Bantry. The post office will be closed but you can telephone from the hotel.'

Penny had no idea what a creamery lorry might be but she desperately wanted her mother's cable.

'Oh, dear, I hope the creamery lorry will be quick, we do so dreadfully want to know how Daddy is.'

'Holding his own,' Great-Aunt Dymphna shouted. 'I asked the seagulls before I came out. They'll tell me if there's any change.'

'She's as mad as a coot,' Alex whispered to Penny. 'I should think she ought to be in an asylum.'

Penny shivered.

'I do hope other people live close to Reenmore. I don't like us to be alone with her.'

But in Bantry when they stopped to send the cable nobody seemed to think Great-Aunt Dymphna mad. It is true the children understood very little of what was said for they were not used to the Irish brogue, but it was clear from the tone of voice used and the expression on people's faces that what the people of Bantry felt was respect. It came from the man who filled the car up with petrol, and another who put some parcels in the boot.

'Extraordinary!' Alex whispered to Penny when he came out of the hotel. 'When I said "Miss Gareth said it would be all right to send a cable" you'd have thought I had said the Queen had said it was all right.'

'Why, what did they say?' Penny asked.

'It was more the way they said it than what they said, but they told me to write down the message and they would telephone it through right away.'

It was beginning to get dark when they left Bantry but as the children peered out of the windows they could just see purplish mountains, and that the roads had fuchsia hedges instead of ordinary bushes, and that there must be ponds or lakes for often they caught the shimmer of water.

'At least it's awfully pretty,' Penny whispered to Alex. 'Like Mummy said it would be.'

'I can't see how that'll help if she's mad,' Alex whispered back.

Suddenly, without a word of warning, Great-Aunt Dymphna stopped the car.

'We're home.' Then she chuckled. 'I expect you poor little town types thought we'd never make it, but we always do. You'll learn.'

The children stared out of the car windows. Home! They seemed to be in a lonely lane miles from anywhere.

'Get out. Get out,' said Great-Aunt Dymphna. 'There's no drive to the house. It's across that field.'

The children got out. Now they could see that the car had stopped at a gap in a fuchsia hedge, and that on the other side of the hedge there was a field with a rough track running across it.

'Where do you garage your car?' Alex asked.

Great-Aunt Dymphna gave another chuckle.

'There isn't what you mean by a garage, but there's a shed in the field. Too dark to put the car away tonight. Shall leave her where she is until the morning.'

Although the children were used to staying in a caravan they were not used to walking about in the country in the night. On caravan holidays they were always in or near the caravan eating supper or doing something as a family long before it was dark. Now they found they were expected to carry their suitcases across a pitch black field to an invisible house, without even a light to guide them. As well there was no Great-Aunt Dymphna to lead the way for, having said the car would wait where it was until the morning, she had vanished across the field, her cape flapping behind her.

'Horrible old beast!' thought Alex, dragging their cases from the boot. 'She really is insufferable.' But he kept what he felt to himself for out loud all he said was:

'Let's just take the cases we need tonight. We can fetch the others in the morning.'

Alex led the way, carrying his and Naomi's cases, Robin came next, Penny, gripping Naomi's hand, followed the boys.

'I don't wonder nobody brings a telegram here,' said Robin. 'I shouldn't think anybody brings anything. I should think we could all be dead before a doctor comes.'

Alex could have hit him.

'Shut up, you idiot. Of course people come, you heard what she said about a creamery lorry, and there must be a postman, everybody has those.'

'If they're real they do,' Robin agreed, 'but I don't think she is real. I think she's a vampire. I shouldn't wonder if she drank our blood when we're asleep.'

Naomi gave a moan and stumbled against Penny. Penny was sick with fear but she was also angry.

'I should have thought, Robin, one way and another

things were awful enough without you making them worse.'
Then she said to Naomi: 'Don't listen to him, darling, you'll
feel quite different after a hot bath and then I'll give you
your supper in bed.'

Naomi was clear about that.

'Not if it means my being alone for one single minute you
won't.'

'Even if you don't think she's a vampire,' said Robin, 'I
vote we keep our windows shut just in case, that's the way
they get in.'

Alex put down the suitcases and turned to face Robin.

'Will you shut up. You know you promised you'd obey
me.'

Robin was outraged.

'Mummy said I was to do what you and Penny told me,
but she didn't say I wasn't to talk.'

Alex's voice was fierce.

'Well, I'm telling you to shut up and that's an order.'

After that, except for angry mutters from Robin they
finished crossing the field in silence. It was then they saw a
light. It was very feeble but it was a light.

'Thank goodness,' said Penny. 'This suitcase weighs a ton.'

The light was a candle held by Great-Aunt Dymphna.

'Come along, come along. Thought I'd lost you.'

The children followed Great-Aunt Dymphna into the
house and thankfully put down their suitcases. Great-Aunt
Dymphna was lighting four more candles, each was stuck to
a saucer.

'You can't see much in this light but up those stairs and
turn left you'll come to a door, that's the west wing. It's all
yours.'

Penny was standing beside Alex, she gripped his hand.

'Ask about supper?' she whispered.

'Thank you very much,' Alex said, trying desperately to
sound polite. 'Do we come down for supper?'

'Supper!' Great-Aunt Dymphna sounded as though she
was trying out a new word. 'Oh! When you get to the west
wing at the end of the passage there are back stairs. At the

bottom there is a kitchen, you'll find all you need there. Good night.'

In the flickering light of their candles the children humped their cases up the stairs, which were wide and uncarpeted. At the top of the stairs they turned left as directed and sure enough they came to a heavy door. Alex opened it but when they were all through it closed creakingly behind them. Penny shivered.

'How shall we know which rooms are for us?'

The question answered itself for on the first door they came to a piece of paper was pinned. It said 'Penelope.' They all walked in.

The room was almost bare, it had no carpet, no curtains and no pictures, but there was a large unmade double bed with one pillow, two blankets, two sheets and one pillowcase lying on it. In a corner there was a mahogany cupboard. It was so awful a bedroom Penny said nothing except:

'Let's look at the other rooms.'

Alex's room was next, it was just like Penny's except that his bed was single and one of its legs had a bit broken off it, so the bed was propped up on two books. He had no cupboard but he had a cheap yellow chest of drawers. In Robin's room there was also a single bed and what must once have been a rather grand hanging cupboard but the door was off its hinges. Naomi's room, which was the far side of the bathroom, had a single bed, a rickety chest of drawers, which leant drunkenly against the wall, but she had a picture, it was of the devil pushing a man into a cauldron.

Everything was so truly terrible it was no good pretending it was not so Alex did not try, instead he said:

'Just dump the cases and we'll see what's for supper.'

The mention of supper was too much for Naomi, she sat on the floor and howled.

'I couldn't eat anything. I'm frightened. I won't sleep alone in this horrible room. Nobody is going to make me.'

Penny knelt down beside her and hugged her.

'Of course you shan't sleep alone, you can sleep with me in my bed, it's enormous.'

'She's a witch,' Naomi howled. 'I know she's a witch. Oh, Penny, I'm so frightened!'

'It's all right, Naomi,' said Alex. 'Of course she isn't a witch, you'll be all right in the morning, you're only tired.'

But Naomi would not be comforted.

'If she's not a witch she's a vampire, like Robin said.'

Penny tried to laugh.

'Don't be so silly, darling, there aren't such things . . .'

Then she broke off for at that moment something banged against the window before it flew off into the night.

7

Breakfast

ALEX and Penny talked in whispers after Robin and Naomi had gone to sleep – Naomi in Penny's bed and they had moved Robin's bed into Alex's room. They sat on Penny's bed eating some chocolate that Alex had found in a coat pocket.

'What do you suppose that was at the window?' Penny asked.

Alex was rather ashamed at how scared he had been.

'An owl or a bat, I suppose. It was just it happening when Naomi was carrying on about witches and that ass Robin's vampires that made it so queer.'

Penny shivered.

'It was awful, I was nearly sick. What do you think we ought to do? I mean, Mummy wouldn't let us stay here one minute if she knew what Great-Aunt Dymphna was like, and what her house is like.'

Alex licked the last taste of chocolate off his fingers.

'There's nothing we can do. It will be pretty awful for you and me for we'll have to try and make life bearable for Robin and Naomi, but I should think they'll be all right when they settle down.'

'I don't see how you and I can make things bearable,' said Penny. 'Just look at these rooms, they're slums, and have you tried the bath water?'

Alex had, and he had almost laughed remembering Penny saying to Naomi, 'You'll feel quite different after a hot bath,' for there was only one bath tap, out of which came golden brown ice-cold water.

'I expect we can keep clean with kettles and, though the rooms are bare, I suppose they have all we need. I mean, beds and bedclothes and there are cupboards of a sort.'

Penny did not answer that. Her room, lit by a flickering candle, looked inexpressibly grim and the thought of kettles for washing, to someone who had always had hot water from taps, was not cheering. It was all she could do not to cry, especially when she thought of how dreadfully far away their mother was and how ill their father.

'The first thing tomorrow we must find out about the creamery lorry which will bring the cable. I can't think where it passes here, I suppose we'll sit in that lane where we left the car and wait for it passing.'

Depression was creeping over Alex like a fog, but it was no good saying so. He got up.

'We better go to bed I suppose. Shout if you want anything.'

'Can I help you make your bed?'

Alex sounded cross to hide how miserable he was.

'Of course not.' Then feeling mean, he added: 'I bet it will all look better in the morning.'

And it did look better. Probably because the children were hungry they all woke early and at once went to the windows to see where they were. The view was breathtakingly lovely. The windows were in what must be the front of the house for they looked over the field to the lane where the car was parked. The house was evidently high for below them lay a great stretch of country leading to a sheet of water. The water was obviously sea for there were rocks covered in seaweed, some of it of a startling golden yellow colour, but it wasn't like sea in England with an ordinary beach but more like photographs they had seen of a Norwegian fjord, a sort of neck of water with land on both sides of it.

'My goodness!' said Penny. 'Whatever the house is like inside it's gorgeous outside.'

'Should you think it would be all right just for today if we had breakfast in our dressing--gowns?' Alex suggested. 'I'm starving.'

He had only to mention breakfast and without further words the other three were following him along the passage where, as Great-Aunt Dymphna had promised, there were back stairs leading to a kitchen.

The kitchen was enormous, dominated by a huge black cooking range. In the middle of the room was a bare table. On a dresser there were a few plates and cups and saucers. Penny pointed to the range.

'That's to cook on, I mean people used to, I've seen pictures of them, I don't think Great-Aunt Dymphna can use it, there must be something easier.'

'Where's the fridge?' Naomi asked.

Robin made a discovery. He had opened a back door and there on the step was a basket of eggs, a pat of butter and a jug of milk.

'Oh, jubilate!' said Penny. 'Now, where do we boil the eggs?'

The answer was a greasy little gas stove in the scullery off the kitchen. Gas was not apparently laid on but there was a big container of gas standing beside it and it lit quite naturally when, after a search, the children found some matches. No water came out of the scullery taps when they turned them on, but they found some water which looked clean in a pail, and they found a large battered saucepan and a kettle.

'It's not awfully clean,' said Alex, sniffing the saucepan, 'but it won't matter for boiled eggs. How many could you eat?'

'Do you think we ought to eat more than one each?' Penny said nervously. 'I mean, we don't know what Great-Aunt Dymphna is cooking for lunch. She may want them for a Yorkshire pudding or something like that. I know that takes lots of eggs, I've heard Mummy say so.'

Alex would not listen to her.

'I don't care what they are wanted for, we're having supper as well as breakfast. You remember she said we'd find all we needed in the kitchen.'

'But where?' Robin asked, standing on tip-toe to peer into a cupboard. 'She didn't mean those eggs for supper as they were outside, there must be something inside.'

'You cook the eggs,' Alex told Penny, 'and we'll see what else there is.'

Back in the enormous kitchen they found a door they had missed which led into a larder. It was quite big and very cold. On a shelf was a plate of sausages and a cold ham and in a crock a loaf of bread. There was also a basin full of very green apples. On a lower shelf there were some jam jars and pots, each filled with what looked like dead leaves, and there was a plate of dried things that looked yellow and powdery. Robin sniffed at what was on the plate.

'I believe they're toadstools.'

Alex took the loaf.

'Don't be an ass, toadstools are poison. Now we want plates and knives and things like that.'

It was Naomi who found the tea and the teapot. The tea was in a tin marked 'Mrs O'Brien' and it was on the range with an old black teapot beside it. It was quite by accident they found the knives and forks for they were in a wooden box on the floor, and Robin only discovered them because he fell over the box. No amount of searching produced a table-cloth or a bread board or salt, but nobody cared, they just stood round Penny, drooling with hunger waiting for the eggs to be cooked.

'I'm sorry they're so long,' Penny said, 'but the saucepan's big and I expect I put in too much water. I think Mummy only puts a little in.'

At last the eggs were boiled, though rather runny, and the children sat down to breakfast. In spite of the eggs not being quite right it was a delicious meal. The bread was not like any bread they had eaten before, but they loved it and, spread with lashings of the excellent butter, it was fine.

'As soon as I've got clothes on,' said Penny, 'I shall go and watch for that creamery lorry.'

Alex looked at their cups and plates.

'I suppose we ought to wash up this lot.'

'Oh, bother!' said Penny. 'I suppose I ought to have put the kettle on again. It really is insufferable there being no hot water in the taps. I can't think how Great-Aunt Dymphna can bear it.'

'Can't you, indeed, miss! Well I can promise you she bears it very well indeed.'

It was one of the things that was particularly startling about Great-Aunt Dymphna, the way she came and went without making a sound. The children got nervously to their feet. Great-Aunt Dymphna, they noticed, was dressed

exactly as she had been the day before, except now she had added a large black and red check apron to her outfit.

'Good morning,' each child said and then, unable to think of anything more, stared stupidly at their great-aunt.

'I suppose you'll want to find that creamery lorry,' said Great-Aunt Dymphna. 'No need but I suppose you believe there is more truth in a cable than in what my seagulls tell me. I had a word with them this morning – no change, your father's holding his own. Slept well, I hope, beds comfortable? Had a good breakfast?'

It was clear Great-Aunt Dymphna was going and this made Penny brave.

'Where and when does the creamery lorry go past?'

'Any time, but if there's a cable they'll give it to Mrs O'Brien.'

'The one on the tea caddy?' Robin asked.

'That's right. She will drink tea. Poison and so I've told her. You drink it I suppose?'

'Robin has mostly milk and Naomi milk only,' said Alex.

Penny, feeling that at any moment Great-Aunt Dymphna would disappear out of the back door, stood in front of her.

'Where do we find Mrs O'Brien?'

'End of the lane. Can't miss it.'

Alex joined Penny. Great-Aunt Dymphna must not be allowed to disappear until he had asked her some questions.

'Could you tell us about meals and things? What time is lunch?'

Great-Aunt Dymphna looked at Alex as if he was a freak. 'When you're hungry of course. When else should it be?'

'But who cooks it?' Penny asked.

'Who?' That clearly flummoxed Great-Aunt Dymphna. 'Why you,' she said at last. 'Who else?'

'But Penny can't cook, Great-Aunt Dymphna,' said Naomi.

'Then she must learn, mustn't she?' Great-Aunt Dymphna chuckled. 'And I think we must arrange something about my name. Great-Aunt Dymphna is a mouthful. Aunt Dymphna will do. Any more questions?'

There were hundreds, the point was where to start. Penny looked desperately at Alex.

'Food,' she whispered. 'Where do we get it?'

Alex nodded.

'I know there's a ham in the cupboard and some sausages but ordinarily where does food come from?'

Aunt Dymphna sounded impatient.

'Bless the boy, where should it come from? Fish from the sea and there are prawns in the bay. You'll find rods, lines and nets in the outhouse.'

'But meat?' Alex asked.

'Very unhealthy. Never touch it myself. If you must have it ask Mrs O'Brien. Now is that all?'

'No, it isn't,' said Penny. 'Aren't there any rules? I mean when do you want us to be in and where do we have meals?'

'And where are the shops?' Robin asked.

'And where do we find you when we want you?' said Alex.

Aunt Dymphna seemed to grow in height until she towered over the children.

'You have a whole wing of the house to yourselves. This magnificent kitchen. The glorious world outside to play in. All that the earth brings forth to feed you, and you stand there asking foolish questions until my head reels. Help yourselves, children, help yourselves.' Then, flapping her cloak as if to shoo off a clutter of chickens, she was gone.

8

House Viewing

THE breakfast dishes washed up, the beds made, the cases fetched by Alex from the car, which was still standing in the lane, the children, dressed in jeans and rubber boots, set off up the lane to find Mrs O'Brien.

As Aunt Dymphna had said, it was impossible to miss Mrs O'Brien's, hers was the only other house in the lane. It seemed to be a small farm for chickens were clucking about the yard and there were a few cows in a field.

'I do hope we understand what she says,' said Penny anxiously. 'I didn't understand much in Bantry.'

They had meant to knock on the door but Mrs O'Brien came out to meet them. She was a dark-haired rather fat woman. She beamed at the children and to their relief spoke without too much of a brogue.

'So you got here all right, and I hope found everything to your liking.'

Penny was too anxious to be polite.

'Has the creamery van left a cable?'

'It has not but I will be bringing it down when it comes.'

Naomi caught hold of Mrs O'Brien's apron.

'Aunt Dymphna thinks the seagulls tell her how Daddy is, do you think they do?'

Mrs O'Brien was evidently a kind woman. She stroked Naomi's curls.

'It's beautiful the hair you have. Your Auntie has a powerful way with seagulls.'

'But it's nonsense to say they bring messages,' Alex protested.

'Maybe it is and maybe it is not. There is no saying what a seagull knows. You should hear them scream when there has been a wreck.'

That sounded horrible so Penny changed the subject.

'Do you come to Reenmore often? We saw your name on the tea caddy.'

Mrs O'Brien laughed.

'Your Auntie's a strange old one about her food, she won't take a sup of tea. I come down to give a clean up now and again, but I must have my tea so it's my own caddy she is keeping for me.'

'I'm afraid we are using it because it's the only tea there is,' said Penny. 'I don't know how we're going to manage. Aunt Dymphna says I must cook but I can't.'

Penny hoped Mrs O'Brien would tell her not to worry, she would do the cooking, but nothing like that happened.

'You will learn, there is nothing so hard to it. When you want to know how to do something you can ask me. There is no need to be making pastry or fancy stuff right away.'

'But where does food come from?' Robin asked. 'Where are shops, I mean, for ice-cream and sweets?'

Mrs O'Brien pointed in the direction of the sea.

'There is a small shop maybe a mile down the road.'

'And meat? What happens about that?' Alex asked.

'It will be coming out by the bus or maybe a van.'

Alex liked Mrs O'Brien but he thought she was slow at explaining.

'But where from and who orders it?'

Mrs O'Brien was clearly puzzled for she could see nothing for Alex to worry about.

'There is a big ham in the larder for I put it there myself. Your Auntie brought sausages out from the town, there is a sack of potatoes beyond the back door – why are you wanting meat?'

'I'm not – I mean not now, but presently we'll want some.'

Mrs O'Brien laughed.

'Hark at the boy! You have a ham for your dinner with a potato in its jacket – a meal for a prince that will be. For supper you have the sausages, very good they are with tatties mashed with butter, and there is apples to cook. When something more is needed you will ask me.'

In the lane outside Mrs O'Brien's house the children held a consultation.

'I suppose she's right. Ham will do for lunch,' said Penny, 'and thank goodness I don't have to cook it, but I'm certain there are things we need right away.'

Naomi was still tired after the strain of the day before. She was not as a rule a whiny child but she whined now.

'I want to go and play on the beach.'

Alex felt a whining Naomi was the last straw.

'Well, you can't. There's tons to do and nobody to take you.'

Naomi's mouth turned down at the corners so Penny hurriedly intervened.

'I tell you what, let's go back to the house and make out a list of things we must have. Then why don't you, Alex, and Naomi try and find that shop and see what you can buy?'

'And me,' said Robin. 'It's me that keeps asking about the shop.'

Alex looked at Penny.

'He may as well come too, don't you think?'

The last thing Penny wanted was to be left alone in Reenmore but she could not say so. One hint that she was scared and they would have Naomi crying again.

'All right,' she agreed. 'I just thought it would be nice to have someone to help.'

'Help with what?' Robin asked. 'There's only potatoes in their jackets.'

A further search of the kitchen and the near-by rooms brought a surprising collection of necessities to light. Aunt Dymphna might keep things in odd places but she had most of the things found in ordinary kitchens.

'I tell you what would be nice if the shop has them,' Penny said to Alex. 'Tomatoes and a lettuce. Mummy always buys them when we're eating anything cold.'

Alex was a bit worried about spending their own money on food, but he did not know what arrangement their mother had made with Aunt Dymphna. Still, just for today, it could not be helped. So calling Robin and Naomi he went off in search of the shop.

Penny came to the front door and watched the other three cross the field and disappear through the gap in the hedge. Then she looked at her watch. It was still quite early, not yet half past ten. There was no need to bother about the potatoes yet. Instead she would explore. There must be another way out of the house than through the field, probably through the back door. Cautiously, in case Aunt Dymphna was about, she opened the first door on her right.

Penny found herself in the dustiest room she had ever seen. Cobwebs hung from the ceiling and dust lay like moss on every place it could lodge. The walls must once have been papered for remains of a tattered red-striped paper still clung in places. The only furniture was a wobbly little table and one rickety kitchen chair.

'Two old chairs and half a candle—
One old jug without a handle,—
These were all his worldly goods:
In the middle of the woods,
Of the Yonghy-Bonghy-Bò.'

Penny swung round. Really it was intolerable the way
Aunt Dymphna crept about!

'Goodness, you made me jump!'

'But you were thinking of the Yonghy-Bonghy-Bò,
weren't you?'

Penny had no idea what Aunt Dymphna was talking
about.

'Who?'

Aunt Dymphna for a moment seemed silenced, then she
said in a fierce whisper:

'Can it be that a niece of mine has been brought up without meeting the Yonghy-Bonghy-Bò? What is education
coming to? Are you a savage, child?'

Penny thought that a bit much from someone who lived
far more like a savage than anyone she had ever met.

'Of course I'm not. If it's something you think I ought to
have read about – well, I haven't.'

Aunt Dymphna spoke into space and the person she spoke
to was the children's father.

'Oh, John! John! What have they done to you? Did
you never tell this child about the Coast of Coromandel?'

Penny was not allowing that.

'Daddy's always terribly busy. He hasn't time to talk
about Geography to us, and anyway we learn that at school.'

Aunt Dymphna did not seem to hear. She sort of danced
round the room, her cloak as it flew behind her raising a
cloud of dust; as she moved she chanted:

'On the Coast of Coromandel
Where the early pumpkins blow,
In the middle of the woods
Lived the Yonghy-Bonghy-Bò
Two old chairs and half a candle—
One old jug without a handle,—

These were all his worldly goods:
In the middle of the woods,
These were all the worldly goods,
Of the Yonghy-Bonghy-Bò.'

Aunt Dymphna was back beside Penny. She pointed to the
rickety little table and the shabby kitchen chair. 'This is
where I eat so you see I do resemble the Yonghy-Bonghy-
Bò.'

If all the Yonghy-Bonghy-Bò had was two old chairs and
half a candle and one old jug without a handle Penny could
see the whole house might have belonged to him; however,
she could not say that so instead she explained why she was
there.

'I was exploring. I hope you don't mind.'

Aunt Dymphna flapped her cloak as if she were about to
fly, she sounded excited.

'Splendid! Splendid! We'll explore together.'

It was the oddest house. Everywhere thick with dust. The
floor piled with books. Nowhere much furniture and, what
there was, terribly shabby. But Aunt Dymphna did not
seem to notice dirt or shabbiness or books on the floor, she
showed off each room as if it were splendidly furnished.

'This is my drawing-room,' she explained, throwing open
a door across the passage from the dining-room. 'A lovely
room, is it not?'

Penny tried to find something nice to say but she could
not. It was to her the worst room she had seen yet for it was
more furnished and, therefore, more depressing. There were
tattered remnants of what once had been gold satin curtains.
There was an awful old carpet on the floor full of holes.
There were several chairs falling to bits, with stuffing and
springs coming out, and most of them had lost a leg. There
were broken tables covered in broken ornaments. In one
place a mass of wires hung out of the wall where once there
must have been a bell. Penny remembered something she
had heard her mother say.

'Aren't you afraid of moths?'

'Never underrate moths,' said Aunt Dymphna. 'They can be very pleasant when you get to know them.'

No room was as bad as the drawing-room but Penny found them all depressing. The little drawing-room, the study, the breakfast-room, the best bedroom, the spare rooms.

'I don't myself use the west wing,' Aunt Dymphna explained. 'But I opened the bedroom floor for you children. I felt you would prefer it to these more formally furnished apartments.'

Penny stared at the bedroom they were in, which was empty except for a pile of books and a broken statute festooned with cobwebs. Certainly their rooms were better than this, for, apart from having beds in them, they were reasonably clean. Poor old thing, she thought. She's hopelessly mad. Out loud she said gently:

'I'm sure we shall be happier in the west wing.'

Aunt Dymphna was at the window. She licked her finger and cleaned a space amongst the dust and cobwebs so that she could see out. She beckoned to Penny. They were looking at the field they crossed to reach the lane.

'This was my drive. Beautiful with shrubs and rhododendrons but I could not afford the gardeners so I gave it back. I think it prefers to live wild.'

Now that it was pointed out Penny saw that the field had the remains of shrubs and bushes on either side of the path. That reminded her about the back door.

'Is there another way out? I mean, Mrs O'Brien brought the eggs to the back door.'

Aunt Dymphna made one of her bird-like swoops.

'Come along. Come along. I will show you.'

The back door opened on to what must once many years before have been a garden. There were still the shapes of beds though there was nothing but weeds in them. Aunt Dymphna led the way up a path past a revolting garbage heap until they came to a small broken gate, and there below them lay Mrs O'Brien's farm. But there was no way to reach it.

'How do you get down to it?' Penny asked.

Aunt Dymphna seemed surprised.

'You don't. But she comes up, which is all that matters.'

'But if she can get up we must be able to get down,' Penny protested.

Aunt Dymphna was gathering her cape round her, preparing to return to the house.

'That is a fallacy, child. Too many people believe there is always a way down if there is a way up and vice versa, there is not. I shall not be here for the rest of the day. Enjoy yourself.'

Penny, returning alone to the kitchen to clean potatoes for lunch, muttered as she opened the back door: 'Enjoy yourself! I'd love to know how I'm going to do that.' She might have muttered more only in the kitchen a surprise was waiting for her. At the table a strange boy was sitting eating their ham. He was wearing black glasses.

9

The Shop

ALEX, Robin and Naomi enjoyed their walk to the shop.
They went up the lane past Mrs O'Brien's and then turned
down another lane that led to the sea. It was a nice pausing
sort of walk, there was so much to look at. A little bog full
of odd plants and queer bright-coloured moss. Blackberry
hedges on the chance of an early blackberry. A little lake
on which floated water-lilies.

'If only it wasn't that Aunt Dymphna is so simply awful,'
said Robin, 'it looks as if we'd like it here.'

Alex was thinking about what Aunt Dymphna had said
about fish in the sea and prawns in the bay, and rods and
lines in the outhouses. There had been so many things to do
on their caravaning holidays that they had not got around
to fishing though other people were doing it. But their father
had said they would fish this year in Scotland. Alex could
not remember exactly what was said but he seemed to think
there had been something about licences for fishing. It
might be fun to fish and certainly a help if you caught anything, but who would know about licences? Certainly not
Aunt Dymphna. How odd it was to have no responsible
grown-ups to arrange things.

The shop when they reached it was not like any shop they
had been in before. There were the usual shelves full of
things to buy, but as well drinks were served. Because of the
drinks there was a bench to sit on against the wall. The
shop had several people in it buying or drinking and they
were all talking, but when the children came in the talking
stopped and everybody looked at them. This did not dis-
courage either Robin or Naomi, who were hungry after the
walk. A red-haired girl was serving behind the counter.
Naomi smiled at her for she thought she looked nice.

'Do you sell sweets and ice-cream?'

The girl leant across the counter.

'We have the sweets but no ice-cream.'

'Oh, goodness!' said Robin. 'I was afraid of that. Does a van come round selling ices?'

Everyone in the shop laughed.

'You will be from England no doubt?' one of the customers asked him.

Robin nodded.

'From London. We are staying at a house called Reenmore, with our great-aunt.'

Alex, who had been looking to see what was for sale, decided to interrupt Robin, for being a talkative sort of boy he would say anything that came into his head to anybody.

'Do you sell tomatoes, please?'

The girl took a tin of tomatoes off the shelf and put it on the counter in front of Alex, but she and everybody else were looking at Robin.

'Reenmore, is it,' a man sitting on a bench drinking beer said. 'Now that is a queer old house.'

'Isn't it just,' Robin agreed, 'but our great-aunt is even queerer. I think she's a vampire.'

'I think she's a witch,' Naomi broke in. 'Do you know, last night I'm absolutely certain she banged against my bedroom window riding on a broomstick. Alex – that's him' – she nodded in Alex's direction, 'said it was an owl or a bat but Robin and me didn't believe him, and I don't believe Penny did either. Penny is our big sister, she's at Reenmore cooking potatoes.'

Alex was crimson with shame. Probably all these people were friends of Aunt Dymphna. Suppose they told her what Naomi and Robin had said.

'Shut up!' he said. 'Nobody's interested.' Then he turned to the girl behind the counter. 'How much are these tomatoes? I'll take them, please.'

But Alex's hope of silencing the other two failed for it seemed everybody in the shop was interested and those who were strangers and did not know about Reenmore or Aunt Dymphna were enlightened by neighbours.

'She's a strange old one who lives up beyond.'

'A real old wreck of a place it is.'

A man with twinkling eyes asked Naomi:

'Would there be a black cat now to ride on the broomstick?'

Naomi thought about that.

'I suppose there should be, of course we haven't seen everything yet because we only got here last night, but we haven't met a cat.'

'I'll have this tin, thank you,' Alex said again to the girl, 'and we want some sweets and things. What will you have, Naomi, I've got your pocket money?'

That did make Naomi and Robin turn their attention to the counter, but as the girl laid out sweets and chocolates for them to look at Robin went on talking.

'Food's awfully queer at Reenmore,' he told the shop. 'I mean, Penny is supposed to cook it and she can't cook, so I expect everything will have to be cold except eggs, she can boil those. Don't you think we better buy something for tea, Alex? You know there's only bread.'

Alex wanted nothing except to get Robin and Naomi out of the shop.

'All right, but be quick. What do you want? Biscuits?'

Robin and Naomi refused to be hurried.

'Chocolate biscuits are nice for tea but if it's for a pudding as well, which it looks as if it might be, shortbread is good,' said Naomi.

'We didn't have any supper last night,' Robin explained to the company, 'because we were all too scared to go to the kitchen. In case that happens again, Alex, don't you think we better stock up with biscuits?'

Alex would have agreed to almost anything.

'All right, we'll take a packet of ginger, one of chocolate and the shortcake and those chocolates and sweets.' He laid a pound note on the counter. Slowly the girl counted out the change. It was Irish money, which Alex was not yet used to, but he scooped it up without checking and seizing the bag with their purchases marched to the door.

'Come on, you two.'

Robin and Naomi thought that rude. They looked round smiling.

'Good-bye.'

'Good-bye now,' everybody said, and the man with the twinkling eyes added: 'Look out for a black cat, one is sure to be around.'

Crimson in the face Alex strode up the road, the laughter from the shop ringing in his ears.

'What came over you two?' he scolded. 'Telling everybody our business.'

'But they liked hearing,' Robin protested.

'Oh, do go slower,' Naomi panted. 'And I want a Mars bar.'

Alex remembered something his mother said about eating between meals.

'You can't have it now, it will spoil your lunch.'

Naomi was not having that.

'If I don't have a Mars bar I won't have the strength to walk home, and anyway you promised we could go on the beach.'

They were passing some rocks covered in golden flowers beyond which lay the sea. It was not yet twelve, there was no reason why they should go back to Reenmore yet.

'All right,' Alex agreed grudgingly, 'but only for half an hour, and you don't deserve it, nattering like that to complete strangers.'

'And can we have a Mars bar?' Robin asked. 'Truly, we're hungry.'

Alex, now he came to think of it, was hungry too. How stupid and upside-down life had become, turning him at thirteen into a sort of grown-up. What did it matter if, because they ate now, they didn't eat so much ham for lunch?

'Oh, all right.' He put the bag on a rock. 'Help yourselves. I don't care if you're sick.'

Back in Reenmore kitchen Penny was talking to the strange boy.

'Who are you? Haven't I seen you before?'

The boy had a foreign accent.

'Perhaps. I am travelling on the same aeroplane as you.'

Then Penny remembered.

'Of course. You are the boy who was sick and told the stewardess you were being met and then went off all alone. What are you doing here, and who told you that you could eat our ham?'

'I followed you last night.'

'Followed us! How?'

'I am in a taxi at Bantry. I am telling the taxi I was staying in the hotel. After Bantry I am walking for I heard where this house is.'

'Goodness! Aren't you tired? It's miles.'

'Very tired and my feet hurt, also I was hungry. I feared I might faint so I took this ham.'

'But what are you here for?'

The boy lolled in a tired way against the table.

'It is a long story and I would not wish to tell it twice. I think your big brother too should hear when he comes back from the shop.'

'How do you know where Alex has gone?'

The boy sighed at her stupidity.

'I hear, of course. I am hiding. I also see the aunt go out, that is when I dared to come in. Is it possible there is somewhere I could lie down? I am very tired.'

Penny did not know what to do. The boy did look tired, as much as she could see of him behind the dark glasses, and he did not look more than eleven. She could scarcely order him to walk back to Bantry. The house was not hers to invite people into, but inviting could do no harm for goodness knows there was nothing to steal.

'Come along then,' she said ungraciously, 'and do take off those silly glasses.'

The boy stumbled to his feet. Slowly he took off his glasses, eyeing her with an anxious look while he did it. Without the glasses he did look terribly tired and sort of greenish, as if he might be sick like he was on the aeroplane.

'Come along,' she said. 'You can go into the room that was meant for Naomi, but don't make a sound when the others come in. When I get a chance I'll bring Alex to talk to you.'

10

Stephan

IT had sounded easy when she had said it but it proved difficult for Penny to bring Alex to see the strange boy. There seemed no way of getting rid of Robin and Naomi. She tried telling them to go and play outside while she and Alex washed up but Naomi refused.

'I'd rather stay in here with you, I feel safer. Imagine if while we were outside Aunt Dymphna came suddenly like she does. I'm sure I'd scream.'

'Anyway there's only four plates to wash up as there wasn't any pudding,' said Robin in a meaning tone. 'And we ate the tomatoes from the tin and you said you put those awful potatoes in the oven just by themselves, not on a dish or anything.'

The potatoes had been a failure and Penny could not deny it. She had put them in the oven and believed they would roast, but as she neither turned them over nor turned them round they came out almost raw on one side and burnt on the other.

'Don't go on about the potatoes,' said Alex. 'I bet you couldn't have cooked them any better.'

'I bet I could,' Robin retorted. 'I cooked some very good ones on the Guy Fawkes bonfire last year.'

'Well, shut up about them,' said Alex.

Then Naomi, sharing Robin's aggravation because there had been no pudding, remembered the bowl of apples which Penny had hoped they had forgotten.

'Couldn't we have baked apples for supper, with that sort of toffee in the middle of them, like Mummy makes?'

Penny was washing up. She turned in a worried way to Alex who was drying.

'Do you know how you bake an apple?'

Alex dried the last plate.

'Shove it in the oven I should think, but keep turning it round so it cooks all over.'

Penny was against any more baking after her failure with the potatoes.

'Why don't I stew some?'

'How do you do that?' Robin asked.

Penny tried to remember what she had seen her mother do.

'You peel them and cut out the cores, and then I think you just keep boiling them until they're done.'

'Right,' said Alex. 'Peeling apples is something we can all do.'

Penny, feeling frustrated, watched him march off to the kitchen to fetch the apples out of the larder. If only she had managed to explain about the boy Alex would have told Robin and Naomi they couldn't help peel, now they would have them around most of the afternoon. Suppose Aunt Dymphna came back before they had decided what to do with the boy?

The apples were almost all peeled and put in a saucepan before Penny had her brain-wave.

'I tell you what would be nice with these apples. Cream. Robin, would you and Naomi like to go to Mrs O'Brien and see if she could sell us some? You've got the money, haven't you, Alex?'

Alex could see the twenty-five pounds would go much too fast if it was spent on food, which it looked as if it might have to be if, as seemed possible, most of their food came out of tins. But cream was a good idea, stewed apples alone were pretty dull. So he gave Robin some money.

'And you might find out if milk and eggs come every morning and if we ask for more butter when we want it, and of course if the cable has come.'

Robin and Naomi were delighted to fetch cream and had rushed to the door, but Penny followed them.

'If you can do it without making me look too much of a

fool, find out if there's anything extra I ought to know about stewing apples.'

Penny saw Robin and Naomi safely out of the way, then she raced back to Alex.

'Come upstairs quick. I found that boy who was on the aeroplane in the kitchen this morning. He had come in while Aunt Dymphna was showing me the house. He was eating our ham.'

'What awful cheek!'

'Well, never mind that, he had walked out from Bantry, he isn't more than eleven I should think.'

'But what's he doing here?'

'That's what I don't know,' Penny explained. 'He said it was a long story and he would wait to tell it to you too. He looked so awful and said he was so tired I let him lie down in that room that Naomi was meant to have. Come on, we must settle what to do with him before the others get back.'

The boy was asleep when they came into Naomi's room, but the sound of the door opening woke him; he sat up and snatched at his coloured glasses which were lying beside him.

'Don't put those things on again,' said Penny. 'We can't see you properly with them on.'

Alex sat down on the edge of the bed.

'My sister says you broke in here and ate our ham. Why? Who are you?'

The boy got off the bed and walked round the room while he talked.

'I am escaped from a Communist country with my father.'

Alex refused to show how startled he was. Communists! That sounded like police business.

'Where is your father?'

'In England. He believed we are followed. So I am come to Ireland alone. He will come later.'

'But how will he find you?' Penny interrupted. 'I mean, Ireland's a big place.'

'I send a post card last night from Bantry.'

Alex was getting confused.

'What did you write on it? I mean, have you got an address?'

'Yes, here. I listen to you talking at the airport. You say the house is Reenmore and Bantry is the nearest place to telephone.'

'And you wrote all that down on your comic,' said Penny. 'I saw you writing when the stewardess came and talked.'

'That is so,' the boy agreed. 'My father, when he can be sure he is not seen, will ask at a post office if a post card has come. Then, when he can, he will come here to me. I do not think I am followed here, but I do not know.'

'Followed here!' Penny gasped.

Alex spoke firmly.

'We can't keep you here. We are only staying in this house ourselves. I mean, it isn't ours.'

The boy faced them; he looked very frightened.

'Then all is finished.'

Alex refused to believe things were as bad as the boy made out, he might even be making the story up.

'But if you are caught by whoever it is you think is following you – nothing will happen. I mean you only have to call the police.'

The boy looked at Alex as if he were a small child instead of someone older than he was.

'You do not understand. Once my father is a man most important, if it was known he was free and that I, his son, am free, others would join us. Soon we have an army, so those who hate us will not rest until we are dead.'

'Goodness!' said Penny. 'And you think you might have been followed to Ireland? So whoever it is might look for you here?'

Alex thought it sounded like a television thriller. Still, there seemed no doubt the boy believed his story.

'It's no good getting in a state,' he said. 'I suppose you can sleep here for tonight. Our Aunt Dymphna gave us this wing to ourselves so I don't suppose she'll come up. But you'll have to be awfully quiet for if Robin and Naomi – they're the two younger ones – knew you were here they'd tell everybody. They wouldn't mean to but they can't stop talking, especially Robin.'

'I'll sneak things up for you to eat,' said Penny. 'And the bathroom's next door but you can't drink that water because it's dark brown.'

'And if they are out I can perhaps come down?' the boy asked hopefully.

Alex was sure about that.

'Not a hope. You'll have to stay here, we can't have you wandering about the house.'

The boy looked round the bare room.

'It will not be very nice here for long alone.'

That infuriated both Alex and Penny.

'I like that!' said Penny. 'We offer to hide and feed you, and it's awfully difficult to do, and all you say is it won't be nice alone.'

Alex could have shaken the boy.

'You really are an ungrateful little beast. You'll stay in here until we tell you that you can come out, and you'll like it or you can get out now. I'm not in the least sure I believe your story, and I shouldn't be surprised if Penny and I decide you have to go tomorrow. What's your name by the way, and how old are you?'

The boy evidently did not like being told off for he sounded sulky.

'Stephan. I am twelve.'

'Well, Stephan,' Alex went on, 'my sister or I will bring up some tea if we can, but if you don't get it or any other meal you'll know we couldn't make it without being seen. How is it you talk English so well?'

'My father had an English tutor when he was a boy, he is teaching me.'

Penny was standing by the door listening for Robin and Naomi. Now she thought she heard them.

'Quick, there are the others, we must go.'

Alex got up.

'You keep quiet, and whatever you do don't go near the window or somebody's sure to see you.'

Dashing back to the kitchen Penny said:

'What do you think of him?'

Alex shrugged his shoulders.

'He sounds as if he was making it up. But why? It will be sickeningly dull up there. He hasn't even anything to read.'

Penny nodded.

'And only that one awful picture of the devil putting someone in a cauldron to look at.'

Panting they sat down again at the kitchen table and started to peel the last of the apples.

'I feel it's fishy somehow,' Alex whispered. 'But I suppose we can't just turn him out in case it's true.'

Robin and Naomi came flying in with the cream, Robin waving a cablegram.

'We wanted and wanted to open it,' he said, 'but we thought it was mean without both of you.'

Alex tore the cable open. He read it out loud.

'Daddy holding his own this is good news the doctors say Fondest love   Mummy.'

There was quite a pause while they took the message in, then Naomi said in an awed whisper:

'That is almost exactly what Aunt Dymphna's seagulls told her. How did they know?'

11

Toadstools

IT was impossible to get Robin and Naomi out of the way so it was not until both were asleep that Alex and Penny could get any food to Stephan. Alex kept guard while Penny, trembling, went down to the great empty kitchen and cut some cold ham – all the sausages had been eaten – and put a helping of stewed apples and a glass of milk on a tray.

'Beastly tiresome boy,' she thought, peering nervously about the kitchen which, in the light of the candle, was full of flickering shadows. 'We must get rid of him tomorrow, I won't go on doing this. It's bad enough us being here in this horrible house without having to bother about him.'

As both Robin and Naomi were deep asleep Alex, who was in the passage waiting for Penny, came with her to take the tray to Stephan. They found him lying face down on the bed crying.

Alex held the candle in its saucer where he could see Stephan. He gave him a shake.

'What's the matter?'

Stephan sat up, tears rolling down his cheeks.

'It's awful here, and I'm so hungry.'

Penny gave him the tray.

'I'm sorry it's ham again but we'd no excuse to save any sausages for you, but I kept back most of my share of the cream for your apples.'

The boy was evidently ravenous for he started eating at once, and didn't say any more till most of the ham was gone. Then he said:

'Can you leave me that candle? It is terrible in the dark.'

Penny could see it would be if you weren't asleep.

'All right, but I'm afraid you really will have to go

tomorrow. It's impossible to bring things to you with Robin and Naomi around.'

The boy looked scared.

'They must not know. Is it not possible to send them out?'

'Where?' asked Penny.

The boy finished his ham and started on the stewed apples. 'There is beach. Children play on beaches.'

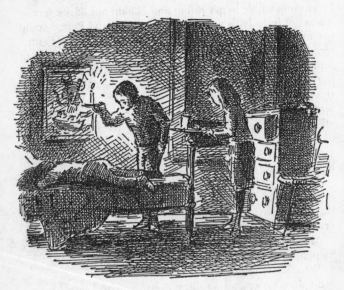

Alex looked at Penny.

'I suppose they could go alone on the beach, it's not dangerous with big waves. I don't think anything could happen to them.'

Penny wanted Stephan out of the house.

'I still don't think it's possible for him to stay here. Suppose Aunt Dymphna caught us carrying trays up, what on earth would she think?'

'Goodness knows,' Alex agreed. 'I expect she'd be furious. Well, it is pretty good cheek putting somebody else up when you are only staying yourselves.'

'If you turn me out I will be killed, I know I will,' said Stephan.

'I do wish you wouldn't talk like that,' said Penny. 'And do buck up and finish eating. Alex has got to take that tray down and wash up, and it's hateful in the kitchen at this time of night.'

Stephan scowled at her.

'You are mean. You think of nothing but yourself. Here's me facing death ...'

'Shut up,' said Alex crossly, 'and get on with it. I'll let you know what Penny and I decide in the morning. While I'm washing up, Penny, get him a pair of my pyjamas, he can't sleep in his clothes.'

Alex fetched Robin's candle for himself and crept downstairs with the tray and washed up in cold water. He saw at once what Penny had complained of, the scullery did look queer in the light of one candle. It looked more than queer, when coming into the kitchen to put the plates away, he saw a face pressed against the window. All faces look nasty pressed flat against a window; this face in the greenish light looked awful. Alex's heart thumped and cold trickles of water ran down his neck. He knew what he ought to do, but it was hard to find the courage to do it. What he wanted to do was race upstairs to his bedroom, shut the door and put something against it. But he was in charge; if someone was outside who should not be, someone probably searching for the boy, he must raise the alarm, call Aunt Dymphna so that she could fetch the police.

They had bolted the kitchen door when they went to bed. There had been some discussion about it for it seemed an odd thing for guests to do but Penny, because of Stephan, had insisted. Now he pulled back the rusty bolts and peered out.

It was Aunt Dymphna who was outside. She came into the kitchen shaking her cape like a bird ruffling its feathers.

'Bolts and bars! Bless my soul, what is going on?' She was carrying a basket. Now she put it on the table. 'We bolt nothing here, boy. Who is there in this gentle country to harm us?' Then she shot a quick look at Alex. 'Have you an enemy?'

Alex hoped he sounded truthful. After all, it was the truth for if there was an enemy it was not his.

'No. No, of course I haven't. I was just scared, you know how faces look when they're pressed against a window.'

Aunt Dymphna opened a drawer and found the remains of another candle. She lit it at Alex's and dripping some wax on to the table stuck the candle to it. Then she tipped out the contents of her basket.

'Fetch the frying pan, will you? I am going to cook my supper.'

Alex stared in horror at what came out of the basket.

'You're not going to eat those! They're toadstools.'

'Edible ones. Delicious. You shall try them. Or have you just had a late supper? Fetch the frying pan, please.'

Alex fetched the frying pan from the scullery.

'No.' Then he remembered he had been seen putting away plates. 'Well, yes. So I'm not hungry.'

Aunt Dymphna chuckled.

'And if you were hungry you wouldn't eat toadstools, would you? You poor town boy, you have no idea of the treat you are missing.'

Alex had no intention of even touching the toadstools. He wondered if Aunt Dymphna was poisoned by them how soon she would be taken ill.

'Are you absolutely sure you ought to eat them?'

Aunt Dymphna chuckled again.

'Bless the boy! Didn't you see the bowl of dried toadstools I left for you in the larder? Delicious in a stew.'

'Oh, is that what they are! Robin thought they might be.'

'Did he now. Sensible boy. And you can use the dried leaves in the jars, they too are delicious and so nourishing.'

Alex suddenly remembered the cable.

'We heard from Mummy. Daddy's holding his own. She says it is good news.'

Aunt Dymphna was slicing her toadstools.

'He is stronger tonight, I heard that from the gulls an hour or two ago.'

'Mad. Raving mad,' thought Alex. Out loud he said:

'Do you want some butter to cook those in?'

Aunt Dymphna looked thoughtfully at the toadstools in the pan.

'Butter. Shall we have butter tonight? How kind of you, dear boy. Yes, just a soupçon.'

Alex thought of Penny waiting for him upstairs. Most likely when he did not come back she would come down to see what had happened to him. Penny was a funny mixture. She could be scared to death but she would still be brave enough to come down. Anyhow, he could not very well leave Aunt Dymphna now, he was her guest and it would be rude to walk out just as she came home to have her supper. He brought what was left of the pat of butter and a knife to the table.

Aunt Dymphna put some butter into the frying pan and led the way into the scullery.

'Wonderful all these modern inventions,' she said as she lit the gas, 'so much simpler than making a fire outside and so much quicker.'

Alex thought the greasy little gas stove was not much of a modern invention, but of course he did not say so. Instead it seemed a good moment to clear up the situation about who paid for the food.

'By the way, I got some things from the shop today.'

Aunt Dymphna put the pan on the stove.

'So you met Bernadette-the-shop – a charming young woman.'

'We didn't know she was called Bernadette, do we pay her or have you an account?'

Aunt Dymphna gave the toadstools a stir with the butter knife.

> 'Down along the rocky shore
>   Some make their home—
> They live on crispy pancakes
>   Of yellow tide-foam;'

As evidently Aunt Dymphna thought that an answer Alex said gently because obviously, apart from the fact she was an aunt and your hostess, you could not be rude to the poor old thing:

'This is something I have to know. You see I have to work out how long the money lasts.'

'Indeed, yes, and so have I. Remember, Alex, what I told you about fish from the sea and prawns in the bay, you may even catch a lobster. You need not pay Bernadette-the-shop, yet again you may. Which is the quickest way to learn, Alex? Do you know? Do I?'

'Silly old coot,' thought Alex, and yet there was something he liked about her. She really was a shocker when it came to answering questions. Suppose he and Penny decided to tell her about Stephan, how would they get her to attend and tell them what to do? He could not think how to answer her so he just stood dumbly by watching the toadstools cook. Oddly they smelt delicious.

Aunt Dymphna lifted the pan off the stove and smelt the toadstools.

'I shall eat these in my room, dear boy. So off you go to bed. But if you should wish to know who lives on crispy pancakes of yellow sea foam look up William Allington. You will find him in one of the rooms. "Up the airy mountain, Down the rushy glen ..." you know.' Then, her cloak streaming behind her and carrying the frying pan and the candle, she was gone.

'I hope she brings the frying pan back,' thought Alex as he relocked the back door. 'I hope, poor old thing, she isn't dead by the morning, but I shouldn't wonder if she is, eating those toadstools.'

12

Wet Breakfast

THE next day was not just wet, it poured as if buckets of water were being tipped out of the sky. The day started badly with a family quarrel. It was bad luck there was a quarrel because it began with good intentions. Robin and Naomi woke up before Alex and Penny. Naomi slipped out of Penny's bed and ran into Robin in the passage.

'Let's surprise the others and cook breakfast,' she whispered.

Robin liked the idea.

'And don't let's just have boiled eggs, I'm sick of those. Let's have fried eggs and what's left of that ham.'

When they were dressed the two sneaked down to the kitchen. They found the frying pan on the dresser.

'What a place to leave it!' said Naomi. 'And not washed up, look, there's still cooking in it.'

Robin smelt the pan.

'The last thing Penny cooked was the sausages. This doesn't smell like sausages, but perhaps it changes smell if you leave it a night.'

Robin got the ham out of the larder.

'My goodness, someone's been eating this, there isn't half as much left as there was after lunch.'

Naomi fetched the eggs.

'Aunt Dymphna, I suppose. She must eat though I can't quite see her doing it – at least not like we do, sitting at a table.'

There were four eggs left, Robin eyed them thoughtfully.

'We have to break them to fry them.'

'I know,' Naomi agreed. 'I've often watched Mummy, she does it on a cup.'

Not successfully the eggs were broken into the frying pan and the remains of the ham, sawed into four rough slices by Robin, put on top of them.

'It's difficult to see which egg is what all mashed up like that,' Robin said, 'but I suppose we can divide it into four. Now I'll go and put it on the stove and then we can lay breakfast.'

'Won't the others be pleased to find it ready,' said Naomi happily.

Robin's idea of lighting the stove was to turn the gas up as high as it would go and leave the frying pan sitting on it. As a result, when a few minutes later Alex and Penny came down, they saw curls of black smoke coming from the scullery, and there was a smell of burning ham.

'You little idiots!' said Penny, snatching the frying pan off the stove. 'What do you think you're doing?'

Alex peered anxiously into the frying pan.

'Did you wash this before you used it?'

Robin and Naomi were furious at being called idiots instead of thanked.

'No, we didn't. Penny hadn't washed it after she cooked the sausages.'

Penny looked despisingly at them.

'Of course I did, you saw me.' Then she looked again at the frying pan. 'Thank goodness nothing is too burned. I expect it will be eatable.'

Alex snatched the pan from her.

'We can't eat that! Do you know what was in it? Aunt Dymphna's toadstools.'

Then Penny remembered, for before he went to bed Alex had told her about his meeting with Aunt Dymphna.

'Ugh! No. Throw it away, Alex.'

Robin was furious.

'You can't throw it away, it's all there is to eat.'

Alex tried to speak in a reasonable voice.

'And whose fault is that? Couldn't you wait until Penny or I came down? I have to throw this away because last night Aunt Dymphna cooked toadstools in this frying pan and if, as you say, it has not been washed the remains are still there. You don't want to die, do you?'

Naomi started to cry.

'Robin and me cooked breakfast as a surprise for you.'

Penny was worried. There had been only four eggs left for she had counted them last night, and very little ham after the helping she had cut for Stephan. What was she to give the family for breakfast, and what about Stephan?

'It was a silly sort of surprise because neither of you can cook.'

Robin was not accepting that.

'It has not seemed to me and Naomi that Miss Penny Gareth is much good at cooking either.'

Penny could have hit him, and besides being angry there was a lump in her throat. She had tried to feed them, she did think they might have realized that and been nice about it.

Alex had scraped everything out of the frying pan into the bucket that they used for a waste bin.

'Instead of arguing about who can cook when we know none of us can, it would be a good thing if we thought about breakfast. I suppose I better put on my mac and go to Mrs O'Brien for eggs.'

'Mrs O'Brien!' said Penny. 'I bet she's not afraid of a little rain.' She unlocked the back door. There on the door-step was a bowl of eggs, a large jug of milk, a small one of cream, a loaf of bread, a new pound of butter and a fresh bucket of drinking water. On a piece of paper under the milk jug was written: 'Bus bringing fish because Friday yours faithfully Mrs O'Brien.'

'Fish!' said Penny in an anguished voice. 'It's probably come straight out of the sea and will need cleaning as well as cooking.'

Alex was so thankful to see the supplies he was quite cheerful again.

'Shove on the saucepan, Penny, and let's have boiled eggs. There's heaps here, who would like two?'

Robin was not a boy to bear a grudge. Cheerfully he

helped lay the table but Naomi was thoroughly upset. Cooking breakfast had been her idea and it had been meant to please the big ones. It was awfully mean of them to be so hateful about it. How were she and Robin to know about the toadstools? If it came to that, how did Alex and Penny know? They had all gone up to bed at the same time. Pottering about the kitchen waiting for the eggs to be cooked she brooded on this. If Alex and Penny had come down to the kitchen after she and Robin were asleep it meant she had been left alone upstairs, which they had absolutely sworn wouldn't happen. When they sat down to breakfast she felt so swollen with grievances she could not keep them to herself.

'I thought you promised you wouldn't leave me alone in the bedroom, Penny.'

Penny was pouring out the tea, her mind on Stephan. Horrible boy, what were they to do? Nobody could turn anybody out in weather like this. She pulled herself back with difficulty to what Naomi was saying.

'What? When were you left?'

Alex wondered if, for a second, Naomi had woken last night while Penny was getting Stephan's tray.

'Get on with your breakfast,' he growled at Naomi. 'Thanks to you it's late enough.'

Naomi put down the teaspoon with which she was eating her egg. She was again near tears.

'I suppose even you and Penny, grand as you think you are, always ordering people about, can't be in two places at once. If you saw Aunt Dymphna cooking toadstools how could you be in bed?'

Alex dared not look at Penny.

'Get on with your egg and don't be tiresome. If you want to know it was I who saw Aunt Dymphna cooking toadstools. I came down for something.'

'Was it to eat ham?' Robin asked. 'We saw some had been eaten.' Penny shot an anxious look at Robin, she did not mean to but she could not help it. Robin saw the look and supposed he had guessed right. 'Fancy it being you sneaking down for something extra, mostly you'd expect it to be me.'

Alex longed to answer that but how could he? If Robin had noticed ham had been eaten it had to be accounted for. That wretched Stephan, what a nuisance he was! He looked at the window against which the rain was lashing. They could not turn him out in this weather, but he would probably get nothing to eat, and serve him right. How could

they feed him with Robin and Naomi around all day?

Penny tried to help by changing the subject.

'Has anybody any idea about what to do today? It doesn't look as if we shall get out.'

'What is there to do?' Naomi whined. 'Mummy wouldn't pack any games because we had so much luggage.'

As Naomi spoke Penny saw her with new eyes and suddenly she was terribly sorry for her. How different she looked from how she looked at home. Nothing could make her curly hair not pretty, but it had acquired in two days a straggling, unbrushed look. She was wearing a pale yellow polo-necked sweater over jeans. She was usually a rather dainty child, now there was a dirty mark on the front of her sweater and her jeans looked as though they had been slept in. Was this really only the second day they had been here? Was it only two mornings ago they had said good-bye to Mummy? Surely no child in two days, even if there was no hot water, could look dirty but that was what Naomi did look – dirty and miserable. 'Poor little scrap,' thought Penny. 'I haven't tried as hard as I might, after all, she's only nine.'

'I know, darling, and the first thing we'll do when we can get to Bantry is to buy you a game. But do you know what we'll do this morning? I'm going to put everything we've got on to boil and then I'm going to give you a hot bath. You can use the water afterwards, Robin.'

Alex was puzzled. Of course he could cook some eggs for Stephan while Penny was bathing Naomi. But how could he get them to him? Penny couldn't have forgotten the bathroom was next door. But Penny had thought things out, and while she and Alex were washing up she sent Robin and Naomi to put the plates away in the kitchen.

'Make him a bowl of bread and milk,' she whispered. 'That'll be food and drink. You can sneak it in while I'm drying Naomi in the bedroom and Robin's in the bath.'

In the kitchen Naomi too was whispering.

'They're hiding something from us, Robin. I don't believe Alex came down to eat ham, it was for something else and we're going to find out what.'

13

Rain

ALEX, having hovered at the top of the back stairs until he saw Robin go into the bathroom, managed to slip unseen along the passage to bring Stephan his bread and milk. Although Alex not only thought Stephan a nuisance but rather a nasty sort of boy, he had taken trouble over the bread and milk.

'I'd better make him a big bowl,' he had thought. 'Poor beast! Goodness knows when he'll get anything more to eat.'

So he cut up several slices of bread into squares, which he seemed to remember was how bread looked in bread and milk. Then, when he had poured the boiling milk on to the bread, he had thought it seemed a bit dull so he had added a dollop of cream and a lot of sugar. So it was with some pride that he presented the bowl to Stephan.

'Here you are,' he whispered. 'You better eat it quickly because it's not as hot as it was. Robin's having a bath so I had to wait for him to go in.'

Stephan was still in bed. While Alex was talking he sat up, stretched and yawned. Then he looked at the bread and milk.

'What is that?'

'Bread and milk, of course. Penny thought it would be the easiest because it's food and drink too.'

Stephan took the bowl and spoon and put a little in his mouth. Then he made a face.

'It is disgusting! I cannot eat such food.'

It was a miracle that Alex remembered sharp-eared Robin in the next room and so did not raise his voice, which it was his instinct to do.

'It's that or nothing,' he hissed. 'And if you want to know,

I think you are the most detestable, ungrateful boy I ever met. I can't think why your country minds you have left it. If you lived here and left we'd be glad.'

Stephan looked sulky, as he seemed always to do when he was told off.

'But I don't like that. Can't you get me a proper breakfast – eggs perhaps and toast?'

Alex took the bowl and spoon away from Stephan.

'I can't because it's been difficult enough to get this to you, now you can just go hungry. Goodness knows when we'll get a chance to bring you anything else. I had hoped to get rid of you today, and we would have if it wasn't so wet. Now you can just stop here and be hungry and I don't care.'

Stephan still looked sulky but also rather scared.

'I can't help not liking bread and milk, I'm used to having the best ...' he checked himself there, 'I mean, things I like.'

Alex, still furious, tiptoed to the door.

'Well you can't have what you like here, just what we bring you. And stay put until you hear Robin and Naomi go downstairs. Don't you dare get dressed until they've gone.'

Penny, having taken a lot of trouble over Naomi's appearance, sent her down to the kitchen while she tidied their bedroom and made the beds.

'When Mrs O'Brien comes ask her if she has any toys or games she could lend just until we buy some.'

Penny had not taken as long over Naomi as she had supposed, so Naomi arrived in the kitchen before Alex had taken the bucket outside to empty. It was not that he had forgotten it but emptying it meant going down the back garden to the garbage heap, and that meant Wellingtons and a mackintosh. He was about to fetch these when Naomi came in.

'My goodness, you do look cleaned up!' he said. Then he remembered Naomi must be kept out of the scullery until he had emptied the bucket. 'I'm just getting my gumboots and mackintosh because I'm emptying the pig bucket. You sit at the table until I come back.'

'Doing what?' Naomi asked. 'I've nothing to play with. Penny said to ask Mrs O'Brien when she comes if her children have any toys.'

'So we will,' Alex agreed. 'But sit quiet for the minute. Penny will murder me if you get mucked up now she's got you so clean.'

Naomi sat down at the table and then a thought struck her. Yesterday nobody had bothered to empty the bucket until after supper, when Alex had made Robin do it. Why was he going out in the rain to do it now? Quick as lightning she darted into the scullery to look at the bucket and was back in her seat at the table before Alex came down.

Naomi watched Alex and the pig bucket slosh out into the rain. Should she go up and tell Robin her news or should she wait until he came down? She had decided to go up and find him when the kitchen door creaked open and there was Aunt Dymphna standing in the doorway. She had slightly changed her dress. Instead of her usual black cloak she was wearing a shawl. It too was black but on it were embroidered flowers which must have once been brightly coloured. Round it hung a matted fringe. On her head she was still wearing a man's tweed hat but she had changed her dress, instead of the shapeless black dress she now wore a shapeless red one which, if anything, made her look more peculiar. On her feet she still wore her boots.

'Goodness, child!' she said briskly. 'Naomi, I take it. Where are the others?'

Naomi's mouth had gone dry with fright. She licked her lips to make her voice come.

'Penny's tidying our room, Robin's having a bath and Alex has gone to empty the pig bucket.'

'Jigs and japers!' said Aunt Dymphna. 'Bless the boy, why empty the bucket in the rain?'

'I think because he didn't want me and Robin to see what was in it.'

'And what pray was that?'

Naomi was still terrified but not as terrified as she had been.

'I thought at first someone had been sick, and then I saw it had been bread and milk – masses of it.'

'Left over from your breakfast no doubt.'

'No, that's what's so odd. We all had eggs . . .' Naomi was going to tell Aunt Dymphna about the thrown away breakfast when she remembered about the toadstools. 'Are you all right? Alex thought a person might be dead if they ate toadstools.'

Aunt Dymphna chuckled.

'Poor, uneducated boy, but he'll learn. What are you doing sitting here? Never sit down on a wet day. Run.'

'Where to?'

Aunt Dymphna flapped her shawl.

'Come along, child. Come along. I'll show you a secret.'

Naomi was appalled but she could see it was no good arguing, so she got up and hurried along behind Aunt Dymphna.

'I would have thought,' she panted, 'you wouldn't mind rain.'

Aunt Dymphna paused to let Naomi catch up, then she gripped one of her hands.

'Why, child? Why?'

Naomi was too frightened to know what she was saying nor was she sure why. She had merely felt that Aunt Dymphna, whatever she was, could never be a mackintosh-umbrella sort of person. Now she looked down and saw Aunt Dymphna's feet.

'Well, you're already wearing Wellingtons.'

'True. True. Great-Aunt Dymphna went to Gloucester, All in a shower of rain. She trod in a puddle, Right up to her middle, And never went there again.'

Quite suddenly Naomi stopped being frightened. An aunt who knew nursery rhymes couldn't be really frightening.

'It was Doctor Foster who went,' she corrected. 'If it's going to be you instead you'll have to find a place to rhyme with Dymphna.'

'Good. Good.' Aunt Dymphna was so pleased she skipped.

'There is a prize for which of us finds the rhyming town first.'

They were in the hall between the dining-room and the drawing-room. Naomi tugged at the hand Aunt Dymphna was holding.

'Good. I like competitions but let's sit down. I can't think when I'm running.'

Aunt Dymphna threw open her dining-room door.

'Come in. Come in. But you are too late, I've won. Great-Aunt Dymphna went to Bol-og-na. All in a shower of rain. Rather an odd way to pronounce it but it will do.'

Naomi looked at her severely.

'You knew it already. That's cheating.' Then, amazed, she stared round her. 'What a terribly dirty room!'

Aunt Dymphna looked round, then she flicked some cob-webs off the fireplace.

'Cobwebs are not dirt, they are fairy lace.'

'That's what you may call them but Mummy wouldn't. She'd call them dirt.' Then Naomi saw a cobweb hanging from the ceiling. 'Though now you mention it they are rather nicely made, but of course I know there aren't such things as fairies.'

Aunt Dymphna clapped her hands to her mouth.

'Quiet, child, quiet. It is safe perhaps to say such things in England, but never, never in Ireland. This is their home.'

Naomi's eyes grew wide with wonder, for it was clear Aunt Dymphna believed what she was saying.

'They live here! Do you mean you've seen them?'

Aunt Dymphna spread out her arms, her shawl fell over them like wings. Almost she sang:

> 'Her skirt was o' the grass-green silk,
> Her mantle o' the velvet fine,
> At ilka tett of her horse's mane
> Hang fifty siller bells and nine.'

Aunt Dymphna put a hand to her ear as if to help her to listen. Then she repeated '"fifty siller bells and nine". Can you hear them, Naomi? Fifty siller bells.'

Naomi was enchanted.

'Almost I think I can. Did you make that up?'

'No. But somebody did of course though nobody knows
who. You can read the whole poem in a book, I'll find it for
you.' Aunt Dymphna knelt down beside the dusty pile of
books, but Naomi stopped her for she thought the books
looked dull.

'You said you'd show me a secret.'

Up jumped Aunt Dymphna and, with her shawl flying behind her, she rushed through the door into the room opposite.

'This is my beautiful, beautiful drawing-room and here is
the surprise.' She pounced towards a broken table on which
was a wooden box. She took from the box a rusty key, fixed
it in place and turned it.

Naomi came to the table and stared at the box. It had a
glass lid inside which was a thing with prickles on it like a
hedgehog. Slowly, as Aunt Dymphna wound it, the prickly

thing began to turn and out came the queerest, gayest little tune.

'It's a musical box,' gasped Naomi. 'I never saw one like that before.'

Aunt Dymphna stopped winding.

'Likely not. Now don't stand about, child. Music is for dancing. Follow me.'

When a few minutes later Alex, Penny and Robin came to look for Naomi they found her and Aunt Dymphna in a cloud of dust dancing a sort of follow-my-leader.

14

Is It a Cat?

MRS O'BRIEN, when she brought the fish, stayed to show Penny how to fry it, and herself prepared and cooked potato chips, which were to be eaten with it.

'I suppose now you always eat meat in London,' she said, 'so you will not have had the chance to cook fish. Why, both my girls could cook the fish for me when they were no more than eight.'

Penny was so glad of Mrs O'Brien's help she could have cried. But she did not need to hear how early Mary and Sheila O'Brien had been able to cook to make her feel inferior for she was feeling that already.

Bathing and tidying Naomi she had realized for the first time what a terrible lot there was about looking after a family she did not know, especially looking after a family in a part of the world where there were so few things to help you. If they had been at home in Royal Crescent she could, she believed, have managed more or less with Mrs Sims coming in to help with the cleaning, and shops full of food that only wanted heating up, and anyway Mrs Maple next door would be sure to have helped. Then there was laundry. When her mother was there lots of things were washed at home, but then there was a washing machine and a spindrier, but if they had been in Medway on their own everything would have gone to the laundry. But what happened here? Mrs O'Brien meant to be helpful but she was so vague.

'A laundry, is it? There is a place does it in Bantry so I am hearing but I never use it myself. It would mean taking it in and fetching it out.'

Penny had noticed that Naomi had gone to bed with dirty feet which had left marks on her sheets.

'How does Aunt Dymphna get her sheets washed?'

Mrs O'Brien shook her head.

'Maybe she is taking them to Bantry or maybe she washes them herself. I know she was borrowing sheets and blankets for you when your mother sent the telegram.'

'Do you know where she borrowed them?'

'I do not. She is a rare old one for keeping herself to herself.'

'Oh, goodness!' Penny had thought. 'I'll have to ask Aunt Dymphna about laundries, but will I get her to answer? She's much more likely to tell me about the Yong-hi Bon-hi-bow however he's spelt.'

It had taken all the saucepans and the kettle to get one hot bath for Naomi and Robin and she and Alex needed baths too. It was really dreadfully difficult to get properly clean in cold, very brown water full of dead leaves, which was all that came out of the bathroom tap.

Then there was food. They had eaten fairly decently so far, but it was going to be a continual struggle to get food that she could cook, and they could not eat cold food every day.

Then there was Stephan. He was a horrible boy but that didn't mean they could just turn him out. If it was not true he might be shot he could certainly die of pneumonia or something if he had to live out of doors.

Above everything there was their father. Whatever she was doing the continual ache of worrying about him was there. If only Mummy was close enough to speak to on the telephone. If only Aunt Dymphna was the sort of person who believed in cables, but what could you do with a person who thought they were told things by seagulls?

Mrs O'Brien tried to be helpful about toys.

'The children never had many and those they had they broke a long while since. But maybe there is an old doll now in the toolshed.'

Naomi was not a child who cared for dolls. What did she play with when she was at home? She was always cutting things out and sticking them together, and she had an enormous farmyard and there were jig-saw puzzles. Now they had asked about toys Penny could see Mrs O'Brien's children were not likely to have anything Naomi wanted. Politely Penny said they would love to borrow the doll, but she knew it would never be played with.

'We must go to Bantry,' she decided. 'To buy things and to send Mummy another cable.'

'When does the bus go to Bantry, Mrs O'Brien?'

'On a Friday but you will not be needing that, your Auntie having that fine big car.'

'But does she often go to Bantry?'

'Not perhaps often but once in a while maybe.'

'For shopping?'

'Maybe it is the way she would be using the shops when she is there, but I would not be thinking that is her reason for going. It is more that she takes a fancy to go like.'

The chips were ready, only needing reheating. The fish was frying and Penny had been told about turning them over, there was no excuse to keep Mrs O'Brien longer. Wistfully she watched her go.

'If only she would come in for an hour or two every day,' she thought, 'I would feel much less despairing.'

Alex and Robin had spent the morning together in what Aunt Dymphna had described as The Outhouse. It was a dilapidated building outside the back door. It had a large hole in the roof so it was not only wet but full of mildew and green slime. But wearing their Wellingtons and mackintoshes the boys were able to paddle around and keep fairly dry.

'What I'm looking for,' Alex explained, 'is those rods, lines and nets Aunt Dymphna said were here.'

'What will we do with them?' Robin asked. 'I mean, won't we need a boat to fish?'

Alex was not going to admit that he did not know.

'I dare say we could hire a boat if we want to,' he said.

For the greater part of the morning the boys found every other sort of thing than fishing tackle. There were boxes and boxes of books; as the boxes were usually cardboard the books were so damp and mildewed they were unreadable.

'I can't think where all these books came from,' said Robin. 'You remember Daddy said Aunt Dymphna escaped from France in a coal boat with all she had in one hold-all, and I must say Reenmore looks like it.'

'I suppose she's bought them here, and she must have bought furniture and things too for the kitchen and the bedrooms.'

Robin kicked at one of the boxes of books, which promptly fell to pieces, spilling the contents on to the floor.

'I should think she's the sort of person who buys all those old books you see on stands outside shops.'

'I should think she goes to sales,' said Alex. 'A boy at school's father is an auctioneer and he said his father sold things in lots, one fairly good thing and the rest rubbish. That was how he got rid of junk nobody wanted.'

The contents of the outhouse made it likely that Alex was right. For it seemed impossible that even Aunt Dymphna had actually chosen all the possessions that she had. There were some hideous broken statues, and a collection of pieces of picture frame tied together with wire. There were piles of bits of furniture. A large wooden box of cups mostly without handles and there were some teapots without spouts. Under a pile of boxes there was a sack containing about twenty stuffed animals and birds, all eaten almost to vanishing point by moths.

'Come on,' Alex said to Robin. 'Let's dump this lot on the rubbish heap. Aunt Dymphna can't want them. In fact I shouldn't think she knows what's in the shed.'

But under the mess they found something that Aunt Dymphna would remember. It was a shabby brown hold-all with an old luggage label tied to it. On the label was written in faded ink: 'Miss Dymphna Gareth. British citizen. In transit for Ireland.'

'My goodness!' said Robin. 'This must be the one she escaped with. No wonder the house has so little in it, she couldn't get much in that.'

Alex looked inside the bag.

'I should think it ought to be in a museum. I mean there

can't be all that number of bags that escaped from France, after all that war was ages ago. Look, there's something in this pocket.' He brought out a postcard. It had a picture on it of the Tower of London. On the other side was written, in ink so old it was turning brown: 'Lily and I feel a bit anxious about you. Do watch the situation, there is always a bed with us. John is such a big boy now. Your affectionate brother, Alfred.'

The boys gazed respectfully at the postcard. Robin said:

'Alfred and Lily were Daddy's father and mother so John is Daddy.'

Alex nodded.

'It's dated September 1939, My goodness, she was lucky she didn't go and stay with them or that bomb would have killed her too.'

'What are you going to do with it?' Robin asked. 'Put it back?'

Alex thought about the postcard.

'No. I'll bring it in and if I get a chance I'll give it to her. I should think she'd like to have it, I mean it's sort of historical.'

It was at the back of a pile of boxes that at length they found the fishing tackle. It was wrapped in some tangled net. Three lines rolled on to frames into which were fastened some rusty fishing hooks, some pieces of fishing rods and two prawning nets, more holes than net.

Even if you are not a fisherman there is something enthralling about the smell and the feel of things to do with fishing. Robin sniffed at the net.

'It's got a sea smell, sort of tar and salt.'

Mrs O'Brien, homeward bound, put her head in at the door.

'The fish is nearly ready. Will you be washing yourselves now, for it is a terrible state you are in from this dirty place.'

Alex came to the door.

'Where did all this stuff come from?'

Mrs O'Brien laughed.

'It is your Auntie can never resist a bargain. Let her just hear the whisper of a sale in some big house and away she is like the wind when it blows from America.'

'I said it was sales,' said Alex. 'I knew because a boy at my school's father is an auctioneer.'

'Look at you, little old sweeps the pair of yous!'

'It's only dust,' said Robin. 'It will wash off in the rain.'

The boys carried the fishing tackle into the kitchen. Penny called out to them to lay the table. Alex looked at their filthy hands.

'We can't touch anything until we wash.'

Robin rubbed his hands on his mackintosh.

'I should think it would brush off.'

It was clear that dirt picked up in the outhouse would not brush off, but Alex did not want Robin going upstairs. He spoke without giving himself time to think.

'Stay down here.'

Robin, half-way towards the back stairs, stopped in amazement. Of course Alex was only a brother but it was not like anyone in authority to stop you washing, mostly they were asking you to do it when you didn't want to.

'Even if I don't wash I've got to take off my mac and boots.'

Alex saw his mistake and tried to cover it.

'What I meant was, cold water won't get this dirt off, we'll have to have a kettle and we can wash down here.'

'What about our macs and boots?'

'We'll have to go out in the rain to get them clean, there's great lengths of cobwebs and stuff stuck to your back. Shove them down in one of the other rooms and then while the kettle's boiling, you might give Naomi a shout and tell her dinner is ready.'

Alex hurried into the scullery.

'Have you managed to get any food up to Stephan?'

Penny, her face crimson from hanging over the stove, gave him a cross look.

'How? With Mrs O'Brien here? And what? All I've got

is fish and it isn't quite cooked, and we couldn't take it up-stairs anyway because it would smell.'

Alex filled the kettle.

'He's had nothing yet today. We'll have to manage something.'

Penny shrugged her shoulders.

'Then you find it.'

Alex saw Penny would be no help so, leaving her to finish cooking the fish, he went to have a look at the larder.

It was queer their larder was never quite bare. Food of a sort was always turning up. Now on a plate, probably put there by Mrs O'Brien, was a pile of bacon slices and some more sausages. There were, too, the rest of the eggs. As it was obvious they could not cook Stephan bacon or sausages Alex picked up the eggs, which gave him an idea. He took the eggs into the scullery.

'I suppose eggs would hard boil just as well in a kettle as in a saucepan, wouldn't they?'

Penny was sorry she had been cross.

'What an awfully good idea. Shove them in, the others won't see them in the kettle, and you can sneak them up to him in your pockets.'

Robin found Naomi in Aunt Dymphna's drawing-room. She had a box full of artificial flowers which she was straightening out. Those she had tidied she was wearing – a wreath of very tired roses round her head, and others as bracelets and round her waist.

'Dinner's ready. Where's Aunt Dymphna?' Robin asked.

'She went away, she didn't say where, but she told me I could play with these.'

'You look an awful ass with those roses on your head.'

Naomi paid no attention to that for she was used to Robin.

'Have you noticed the big ones have a secret?'

'What sort of secret?'

'An eating sort. Like last night Alex coming down to the kitchen again when Aunt Dymphna cooked toadstools. Why did he come, he'd had supper? Then this morning he made masses of bread and milk and then threw it away.'

Robin, who had been wandering round the room, stood still. Now that Naomi was talking about secrets he remembered how odd Alex had been about washing. 'Stay down here,' he had said in an odd way, as if he was fussed about something.

'You might be right, but whatever sort of secret could it be? Who would eat bread and milk? You only have that when you are ill. But whatever it is it's upstairs because Alex tried to stop me going up.'

Naomi took the flowers off her wrists and waist but kept the wreath of roses on her head.

'I should think it's an animal. I wonder if it's a puppy.'

'I don't see why they'd bother to hide that, Aunt Dymphna wouldn't mind our having a puppy, I mean, it couldn't make her house worse. I tell you what, perhaps they've found her cat and are keeping it prisoner.'

'What cat?'

'The one that rides on her broomstick, of course. You remember they asked in the shop if there was a cat.'

Naomi did not like that idea at all.

'I've given up thinking she's a witch, and I don't want to start thinking it again.'

Robin shrugged his shoulders.

'You can think what you like, but if she's a witch she's a witch. Anyway I'm going to find out if the others are hiding her cat. Come on, there's fish for dinner.'

15

Stephan Learns a Lesson

AUNT DYMPHNA, who had changed into her cape, rushed into the kitchen just as the children had finished lunch.

'Who's for a sale – a glorious sale?'

Penny looked at her in horror. Aunt Dymphna was not the sort of person you could say no to, but it was not the kind of day anyone would want to go to sea.

'Won't it be rather rough?'

Aunt Dymphna chuckled.

> 'And everyone said, who saw them go,
> O won't they be soon upset, you know!

That, if you ignoramuses don't know, comes from "The Jumblies" by Edward Lear. What do they teach you these days? No, it's not to sea I am going, my dear Penny, it is to a saleroom.'

Penny, having sampled Aunt Dymphna's driving, was not sure they would be any safer on the road than at sea. Anyway there was the horrible Stephan to think about, and after her effort to tidy Naomi this morning she really did want to clear up generally.

'I don't think I'll go, thank you,' she said. 'But I expect the others would love to.'

Aunt Dymphna was not apparently an ordering-about sort of person for she did not, as Penny was expecting, argue with her but accepted she was not coming and turned to Alex.

'How do you feel about a sale? Nothing like it. There's a rare smell about a saleroom.'

Alex wished he had a chance to discuss things with Penny. He had planned to spend the afternoon mending the prawning nets. He did not think a sale would be much fun, watching Aunt Dymphna buying yet more junk. While he was hesitating Robin said:

'Shall we go near shops? There's lots we need to buy.'

'Shops!' Aunt Dymphna turned the word over on her tongue as if it did not taste very nice. 'Shops. To buy what, Robin?'

'Food,' said Robin. 'Today we had bread and jam for pudding. O.K. for once but not for always. We haven't had a pudding since we got here.'

'Pudding!' Again Aunt Dymphna tried out the word, 'Pudding. "Georgie Porgie, pudding and pie," and what else is needed from a shop?'

'Things to play with,' said Naomi. 'We haven't anything because we couldn't pack much because of overweight on the aeroplane.'

Aunt Dymphna had eyes that seemed to spark when she felt strongly. Now they sparked at Naomi.

'Things to play with! This glorious old house. The magic of Ireland and you say there is nothing to play with!'

Naomi surprised the others by standing up for herself.

'I know you let me play with the flowers, and you turned on your musical box. But what I'm talking about is ordinary things, like my farmyard, it's got over sixty animals, and things like jig-saw puzzles and proper games. Not just things that live in your drawing-room.'

Aunt Dymphna made a disapproving, clicking noise with her tongue.

> 'Higglety, pigglety, pop!
> The dog has eaten the mop;
> The pig's in a hurry,
> The cat's in a flurry,
> Higglety, pigglety, pop!

Now those who are coming come along, come along.'

Aunt Dymphna made her flapping movement with her cape and turned towards the door. Penny bravely laid a hand on her arm.

'Could you give them five minutes? They must tidy and put on their macs and boots.'

Aunt Dymphna looked at Penny's hand as if it surprised her to see it where it was. Then she said, quite gently for her:

'I shall get out my motor car. Then I shall find a dandelion clock. I shall blow slowly but when it has told me the time I shall drive away.'

In the end, after an awful scramble, Alex, Robin and Naomi in their mackintoshes and Wellingtons were splashing across the field. Alex went because of the chance of sending a cable.

'Make her stop at a post office,' Penny said. 'Just tell Mummy we are fine. I'm sure she'll worry if she doesn't hear, and do try and buy some fruit. It'll do in tins if you can't get any fresh.'

They were alone for a minute so Alex whispered:

'After you've fed Stephan you might let him walk about a bit. But don't let him come down in case Mrs O'Brien turns up.'

'And I'd like to tell him he must go tomorrow,' Penny whispered back.

Alex was putting on his cobwebby mackintosh.

'You could threaten to, it might make him behave, but I don't know how we can. I mean, his story might be true.'

Penny watched the family splash across the field and heard their voices in the lane, then the car start up. So Aunt Dymphna had waited. It was frightening to think of the others being driven by her but Penny, as she shut the door, was grateful for an afternoon to herself, and after all she would not be alone for Stephan, however nasty he was, would be in the house. This was only their second whole day at Reenmore and already they all looked not exactly dirty but grubby. If their mother had seen the state of Alex's and Robin's mackintoshes when they went out she would have had a fit. As clear as if she had spoken Penny could hear her say: 'But surely you could have sponged the dust and stuff off them.'

The most important thing was to feed Stephan and now was a good moment to give him a real meal. He could start with hard-boiled eggs, bread and butter and a glass of milk, and while he was eating and drinking she could cook some sausages. Stephan was up and dressed. He looked dreadfully white and his eyes showed he had been crying. He fell on the hard-boiled eggs and bread and butter as if he hadn't had a meal in his life.

'It's your fault if you are hungry,' said Penny. 'You should have eaten the bread and milk. Alex took an awful lot of trouble making it, there was even cream on it.'

It did look as if Stephan had realized that he should have eaten what they brought, for he said much less truculently than usual:

'It was very nasty.'

Penny could hear she sounded like a mistress at school who thought her class was being silly about something.

'Nonsense! It was good food and you should have eaten it. Now, as the others are out, I can cook you some sausages, and would you like a slice of bread and jam for pudding?'

Stephan looked better, but as he felt better he became his usual imperious self.

'Yes, and I will have mashed potatoes with my sausages.'

'You won't, you know. There aren't any.'

'Then cook some.'

How Penny wished he was not so loathsome. It would be more bearable trying to feed him if he was meek and grateful.

'I can't and I wouldn't if I could. As a matter of fact, just before Alex went out we were talking about turning you out.'

Stephan stopped eating. He looked really scared.

'Please, no. Please do not do that.'

'Well, we'll think about it, but you're so difficult to help.'

'I do not mean to be,' Stephan said almost apologetically. 'It is that before people always do what I wish.'

'Life sounds very odd where you come from. I didn't know children were spoilt in Communist countries, which is what you are.'

Stephan looked sulky.

'Not all are. I am different.'

Penny, in disgust, marched to the door.

'You are the most conceited boy I ever met. All the same I'll get you some sausages.'

While Penny was cooking Stephan's sausages she had a splendid idea, which she passed on to him when he was eating.

'Alex said he thought you ought to walk about a bit. You can't go down because a Mrs O'Brien comes in from the farm, but there's nowhere much to walk up here, so I thought you might clean out and tidy Alex and Robin's room.'

Penny might have suggested Stephan should climb Everest he looked so amazed.

'Me! You wish me to clean a room!'

'Yes you, why not? It will be a way of saying "thank you" for all the trouble you are being. I dare say you never thought of saying "thank you" so I'm telling you it's something you ought to do.'

The boy looked sulkier than usual.

'I have never cleaned a room.'

Penny was amazed at herself. She had no idea she could be so tough.

'If you want to know, neither have I. I've helped, of course. But if it comes to that I've never cooked until I came here, and though of course I've helped wash up I mostly dry when I'm at home. But here I've not only cooked and washed up for us but for you. So if I can learn to do things so can you, and you're going to or we won't bring you any supper.'

Back in the kitchen scraping fish bones and skin into the pig bucket before washing up the lunch dishes, Penny discovered telling Stephan what she thought of him had done her good. She was no longer as depressed about herself and her shortcomings as she had been when she was cooking the fish. There was a lot about looking after a house and family she did not know. There was everything about cooking she did not know. But it was true what she had said to Stephan, she could learn and she was going to learn. Feeling almost swollen with good intentions she left the scullery and the kitchen as clean and tidy as those bleak rooms could ever look. She even put on her mackintosh to empty the pig bucket on the rubbish heap. Then, collecting the only brushes, dust-pan and duster that seemed to be in the house she marched up the back stairs. 'Now I'll make that little beast work,' she told herself, 'and if he doesn't he won't even get a slice of bread for supper.'

16

The Sale

AUNT DYMPHNA drove just as terrifyingly as she had on the night they had arrived but somehow it was less frightening. Occasionally Naomi, who was sitting at the back with Robin, as the car skidded across the road narrowly missing a cow did let out a squeak, but mostly she was quite brave. One of the reasons why Aunt Dymphna's driving was less terrifying was that she encouraged the children to join in when she spoke to passing humans and animals.

'Don't leave all the work to me. Dogs who bark at the car want all of us to answer.'

So as dogs rushed out of cottages barking, windows were hurriedly opened and they all leant out and shouted, 'We're going to a sale at Skibbereen, dear,' and at once the dog went quietly home.

Encouraged by Aunt Dymphna Robin and Naomi joined with Aunt Dymphna in shouts of 'Road Hog' at passing cars and bicycles. Alex did not approve of this so, though he said nothing, he looked disgusted.

It was a long drive and it would have seemed terribly long because they could see so little through the driving rain, but Aunt Dymphna cheered the journey up by teaching them a game. She called it 'tags'.

'Couldn't be easier, any fool can play. We each start with ten lives. Count them on your fingers. I say a line of a poem or a nursery rhyme and you, Alex, cap it with another beginning with the first letter of the last word of my quotation, then Naomi caps you and Robin Naomi, and round we go. Each time we can't find a quotation we miss a life. Now I'll start.

> "Up and down the City Road,
> In and out the Eagle."

That's a stiff one, Alex, E's are not easy. I'll give you a chance and give you a third line. "That's the way the money goes" – G is a much better letter.'

Aunt Dymphna slowly counted ten. And just in time Alex remembered something he had heard.

'Grow old along with me.'

'Good boy,' said Aunt Dymphna. 'I'm fond of Browning. Now come along, Naomi. Something begining with an M.'

Naomi had a quick brain for games.

'Mary, Mary, quite contrary.'

Every verse he had ever heard had left Robin's head but Naomi helped him. They were both in the school choir at home and had learnt a Shakespearian song.

'"Come unto these yellow sands,"' she whispered.

Triumphantly Robin produced this as if he had remembered himself.

Round and round they went, Robin losing a life almost at each turn and Alex only managing a quotation about one in three of his chances, until only Aunt Dymphna and Naomi were left in. Aunt Dymphna had lost no lives at all but Naomi had lost eight.

'"I have a smiling face, she said,"' quoted Aunt Dymphna.

'"Sing a song of sixpence,"' Naomi countered.

Aunt Dymphna swerved her car in and out of a herd of cattle.

'"Sing me a song of a lad that is gone," and if that man is not more careful how he directs his animals that line will apply to one of them.'

'"Goosey goosey gander, Whither shall I wander?"' Naomi chanted.

'"We are the music makers, We are the dreamers of dreams,"' Aunt Dymphna quoted.

Naomi thought hard but she seemed to have used up all the Ds she knew.

'One life left,' said Aunt Dymphna. 'Now, what shall I choose? I know. "I will make you brooches and toys for your delight."'

Naomi gave a pleased small squeal.

'I know that one, we learnt it at school.'

'Splendid,' said Aunt Dymphna. 'Then let us call our game a draw. We will recite the poem together alternate lines.'

Naomi shook her head.

'I don't see that's fair. I've got nine against me and you've got none against you.'

Aunt Dymphna missed a bicycle by inches, then scared the unfortunate boy who was riding it even more by shouting 'Road Hog' at him.

'Naomi and I didn't have time to shout too,' said Robin, 'but I wouldn't have because that boy wasn't a Road Hog, he was simply crawling along.'

Aunt Dymphna could sound very imperious when she liked.

'To me anything or anybody who impedes my passage is a Road Hog.' Then, in quite a different voice: 'Come on, Naomi, let us see if we can do justice to the great Robert Louis Stevenson. You start.'

Naomi liked a chance to show off, in a special aggravating reciting voice she began:

'"I will make you brooches and toys for your delight."'

With a terrible jerk Aunt Dymphna stopped the car in the middle of the road. She lowered the window and hung out of it, making a sort of seagull cry. Then she called out: 'Gulls! Gulls! Peck out her eyes. Tear out her liver. Strew her in pieces on the wide ocean. No child should live who dares to speak verse in such a way.'

It was very difficult to tell above the howling of the wind and the lashing of the rain on the windscreen, but it did seem to the children that not so far away they could hear seagulls screeching. Certainly Naomi believed she heard them. She clung to Robin.

'Don't let them get me. Oh, please, don't let them get me.'

Aunt Dymphna closed the window and restarted the car.
'That depends. Say that line again.'

In a trembling voice but with no affectation Naomi repeated the line, ' "I will make you brooches and toys for your delight." '

' "Of bird-song at morning and star-shine at night," ' Aunt Dymphna boomed.

Alex, telling Penny about the recitation afterwards, said it was all he could do not to laugh because Naomi sounded like a frightened mouse reciting a poem with a large, rather savage animal, perhaps a rhinoceros.

Skibbereen had shops and a post office.

'Could you stop here while I send Mummy a cable?' Alex asked.

Aunt Dymphna looked at Alex as if he was a particularly nasty insect.

'Are you made of money, boy? Another cable! To tell your mother what? She knows you are with me in my beautiful home. She knows Ireland is safe and healthy, what could you find to tell her?'

Alex was determined to send the cable but he could not think of a good reason to give Aunt Dymphna for sending it, but Robin had his mind on shops and was not to be put off. He leant over from the back seat, his tuft of hair standing up more than usual. He poked Aunt Dymphna with a finger.

'We told you we had to shop before we started, and I don't see why if we want to send a cable to our mother we shouldn't. You've never met her so we know what she'd like and you don't.'

Alex and Naomi held their breaths. If Aunt Dymphna could ask the seagulls to peck out eyes and other horrors just because you recited in the wrong voice what on earth would she do when someone was almost rude? But Aunt Dymphna was full of surprises. She gave one of her queer rumbling chuckles.

'Tough, eh? Out you get then but be quick, the sale starts in twenty minutes.'

Somehow the cable was sent and the shopping done in quarter of an hour. Naomi had not bought a toy for, if there was a toy shop, she did not find it. She was inclined to grizzle about this but Robin stopped her.

'Shut up! Those seagulls will come if we tell Aunt Dymphna about you.'

The sale was in a big barn. The people who had come to buy could sit on chairs or benches and there was a little platform for the auctioneer. Aunt Dymphna had brought a catalogue with her, and she had marked with a cross the lot she wanted to purchase. She took the children over to look at what she had chosen.

'"Miscellaneous gardening tools,"' she read out from her catalogue. 'The moment I saw that I knew it was just what we needed for final comfort.'

The children gazed at a battered old wheelbarrow filled with rusty trowels and forks, a watering can, about fifty empty seed boxes, a pair of secateurs and, on top, a lot of bass tied together with string.

'Are you going to plant things in your garden?' Alex asked.

Aunt Dymphna evidently thought that a foolish question. 'We are, dear boy. We are. Many hands make light work, you know. And why else, pray, would I be buying the tools if not to use them?'

Seeing all the rubbish Aunt Dymphna had bought and thrown into the outhouse with no intention of using it, Alex thought this a bit thick. However, he did not say so for obviously the less said about gardening the better. Whatever would she expect them to do next? Already Penny was cooking and they were all doing washing up and cleaning. It would be the end if they were expected to make a garden as well.

Aunt Dymphna had not noticed that Alex had not answered for she had seen something which had gripped her interest. It was marked Lot 52. In the catalogue it was described as 'Miscellaneous fittings from schoolroom'. The miscellaneous fittings seemed very like all the other rubbish Aunt Dymphna had bought at past sales: a schoolroom table full of ink marks and carved names, one leg was missing. An assortment of inkpots. Two big piles of school books tied together with string. Four pictures also tied together, the top one of some horrible children dressed in long dresses feeding swans. Then what had caught Aunt Dymphna's eyes? A wooden box with a chessboard marked on it, a game called 'Who knows?' and a little box which Aunt Dymphna pounced on and greeted as an old friend.

'Spillikins,' she said. She opened the box. 'Real ivory spillikins.'

'I think you'd much better buy that lot than the gardening things,' said Robin, 'for I just can't see how we'll get that wheelbarrow home.'

They turned back to the wheelbarrow to have another look at it. It certainly was to ordinary eyes an awkward bit of luggage, but Aunt Dymphna had not ordinary eyes.

'What a wibbley-wobbley lot you are. Discouraged by the

slightest obstacle. And what is wrong with the roof of my car, pray?'

Alex could picture the wheelbarrow swaying on the car roof as Aunt Dymphna drove from side to side. Besides, who was to put it on the roof, and with what would they fix it? They had, as far as he knew, brought no rope with them. But Aunt Dymphna already thought sufficiently poorly of them for Alex not to want to make her opinion even lower – if you could get lower than a wibbley-wobbley lot – so all he said was:

'We shall need something to tie it on.'

Aunt Dymphna looked at him with an amused twinkle in her eyes.

'A profound remark. We shall certainly need something to tie it on. Find it, dear boy, find it.'

Alex looked wretchedly round the barn. Where would you find rope and who would you ask for it? He felt desperately shy and afraid of making a fool of himself. But he was not left alone to search for Robin joined him.

'I expect getting rope will be easy, but I don't see how you tie a wheelbarrow on top of a car.'

'Silly old coot!' Alex growled. 'Who wants all that gardening stuff, anyway?'

'I wouldn't mind gardening,' said Robin, 'if we had time to see anything come up, but of course we won't. I'd rather like to grow radishes. I've never had enough of them.'

A wave of desolation flooded over Alex as Robin spoke. Who could tell how long they might have to stay? If their father lived it might be months before he was fit to travel home. How many more sales would they attend in the pouring rain? How long would the awful Stephan hide in the house? How was he to find out about money for food? Even a big sum like £25 wouldn't last for ever. There was the cheque to cash but that was sure to set Aunt Dymphna off. However, none of these worries could be shared with Robin.

'I suppose we better find the place where all the stuff has been unpacked.'

They found the unpacking place and in a moment Robin

was explaining to a man who seemed to be in charge all about themselves.

'It's our aunt. Well, our great-aunt really, she's buying a wheelbarrow which she thinks we can tied on top of her car.'

'Would your aunt be old Miss Gareth?'

'She would,' Robin agreed. 'Do you know her?'

'She is a strange old one, and there is few have not seen her driving along the road. 'Tis a massacre when she is driving.'

Alex, knowing Robin, tried to stop further talk.

'Could we have some rope?'

"There is none will miss it,' said the man. Then, to Robin: 'You come and look for me when the old lady is wishing to lift the wheelbarrow and I will lend you my arm.'

What seemed to the children hours later, for they were both tired and hungry as Aunt Dymphna did not seem to think about tea, they were on the road home to Reenmore. In the boot, rattling so that they could be heard half a mile away, were the gardening tools. On the seat wedged between Robin and Naomi was the box which Aunt Dymphna said was called a Compendium of Games. On the roof, perilously swaying from side to side, was the wheelbarrow, which had been hauled up there by the man the boys had talked to and some of his friends.

'What a delightful and successful day,' Aunt Dymphna boomed.

Robin nudged Naomi and poked Alex in the back but even he said nothing.

17

Finding Out

PENNY was making a m-over to welcome the travellers home. It was sausages, bacon, eggs and fried bread. For a pudding she asked Alex to open one of the tins of fruit they had brought home. Until they arrived she had been feeling rather pleased with herself for, assisted by a very sulky Stephan, she had worked hard upstairs to get things clean and tidy while the others were away. She had also thought they would be pleased with a m-over for they always liked them at home. But the other three straggled in wet, cross and tired as well as hungry, and were in no mood to like anything. At home their mother would have guessed how they felt and would have said: 'Hot baths all round, you'll feel much better after that, and then come down in your dressing-gowns for supper.'

But here there were no hot baths, and if there had been who wanted to come in a dressing-gown to sit in a huge draughty kitchen with the wind howling outside and the rain lashing at the windows?

'The silly old coot has bought a great wheelbarrow,' Alex grumbled to Penny. 'She made Robin and me get it off the car roof before we came in, and it's sopping in the lane.'

Naomi sounded near tears.

'She said I could come in – but as if I would walk across the field alone! You never know what's about in this place.'

'Such as seagulls,' said Robin, 'waiting to peck out your eyes and tear out your liver and strew you in pieces on the wide ocean.'

Naomi squealed.

'Please don't, Robin, I don't want to remember.'

Alex spoke firmly for no one wanted Naomi howling.

'Cut it out, Robin.'

'Did Aunt Dymphna say that?' Penny asked. 'Why?'

'If you want to know ...' Robin started to explain, but Alex stopped him.

'I said cut it out. Did Mrs O'Brien come in this afternoon, Penny?'

Penny knew what he meant.

'No. I expect we'll get another cable tomorrow.'

Naomi looked at the fruit tin Alex had opened.

'Didn't Mrs O'Brien even come to bring cream? These peaches won't be very nice without.'

That made Penny cross.

"How you do all grumble, it's you who has been out while I've been slaving here. We hardly ever have cream at home, Naomi, and you don't complain. No, Mrs O'Brien didn't bring any, she never came near the house and I don't blame her, who'd want to be out on a day like this?'

Because they were all tired and consequently rather cross the meal was rather a silent one, which was a pity for the m-over was not at all bad, and the peaches very good indeed. When they had finished eating Penny asked Alex to go up with Naomi and Robin.

'There is fresh water in the bathroom for teeth, and make them wash. I'll be up directly I've washed up.'

Alex lit three candles and led the way up the back stairs.

'Now get on with it,' he said to Robin, 'there's nothing to stare at,' but even as he spoke he saw this was not true for Penny had completely changed the look of their bedroom. When he had gone out his and Robin's clothes, which would not go into the little yellow chest of drawers, were hanging out of their suitcases. But now everything was put away in the rather grand hanging cupboard, which Penny had moved from Robin's room. She had even managed, in a kind of way, to get its door back on its hinges. Under the window, neatly stacked on top of each other, were the unpacked suit-cases.

A shout from Naomi and they found the same changes in the girls' room. There Penny had moved the rickety chest of drawers from Naomi's old room, so at last she had been able to unpack properly.

'Goodness!' said Naomi, who was pleased with the change. 'Penny must have worked very hard. Almost the room smells cleaner.'

'It looks all right,' Robin agreed, 'but how did Penny do it I'd like to know? She couldn't have carted this stuff about all alone, somebody must have helped her.'

In a flash Alex guessed the answer. To put Robin off he said the first thing that came into his head.

'I expect Mrs O'Brien did.'

Robin and Naomi gaped at him.

'But you heard Penny say Mrs O'Brien never came,' said Robin.

'Not for a cable, not for cream, not for nothing,' Naomi agreed.

Alex wondered how to warn Penny to think up something to explain. Out loud he said:

'Well, stop nattering and get into bed. Penny will tell you how she did it when she comes up.'

But Robin and Naomi were not put off by that. They met outside the bathroom.

'It couldn't be a cat helped her,' Naomi whispered, 'it's a person.'

Robin nodded, his voice sounded sinister.

'I believe it's a person in the house.'

'Oh, don't!'

'I expect it's one of those ghost things that haunt old houses,' Robin went on: 'I expect the others found it prowling about and hid it so we wouldn't be frightened.'

Naomi was already tired and this thought was too much. She lay on the bathroom floor and howled.

Alex came dashing in.

'Now what's up? I suppose you've scared her, Robin.'

Robin was furious.

'It's you that's scared us. We think you've somebody hidden. Sneaking about with food, and throwing away bread and milk. Naomi and I aren't fools, you know.'

Naomi was beating the floor with her toes.

'He says it's a ghost thing. I hate this house. I want to go home.'

Penny came flying up from the scullery.

'What on earth's up? Do shut up, Naomi, Aunt Dymphna will hear you.'

'I don't care if she does,' Naomi wailed, but she was a little quieter.

Alex looked at Penny.

'It's the furniture. They are saying you couldn't have moved it alone.'

'And you couldn't,' Robin put in. 'And you said Mrs O'Brien didn't come. We knew there was something odd going on. Somebody ate some sausages today besides the ones we had for supper. I counted them when they came and . . .'

'They saw the bread and milk I threw away,' said Alex.

Penny thought quickly. It was an appalling risk telling Robin a secret for he was such a talker. But if the children half knew they had better know the whole story, they certainly could not have Naomi howling the house down.

'We better tell them,' she said. She pulled Naomi up off the floor. 'Get into bed and we'll tell you what the secret is. Then you'll be ashamed you made such a row about nothing.'

But Penny had forgotten that they were just outside the bathroom so Stephan must have heard every word, for if he had been asleep Naomi's howls would have woken him. Now, just as they were moving towards the girls' room, he came into the passage holding his candle. He looked very small in Alex's pyjamas, but he had an odd air of authority about him.

'I was thinking it will not be possible to keep my secret much longer.' Then he turned on Penny. 'It is your fault this has happened, I am telling you to leave the furniture alone.'

'Only because you're so lazy,' Penny retorted. 'You didn't remember they would know it would take two to carry it any more than I did. And you didn't want your chest of drawers moved, which was very dog-in-the-mangerish for you've nothing to put in it.'

Robin was staring at the boy.

'Who are you?'

'Well, don't stand nattering there,' said Alex. 'Suppose Aunt Dymphna came up.'

Penny led Naomi down the passage.

'Come in our room. Then I can put Naomi to bed while we explain.'

While Penny helped Naomi into bed the others sat on the floor. Penny started off by explaining how she had found Stephan. Then Stephan told his story just as he had the first time. At intervals Robin interrupted.

'Why did your father think you were followed? Was it by men with stockings over their faces?'

Stephan did not like being interrupted.

'Of course not. He is recognizing them.'

Robin was amazed when he heard about the postcard sent to England.

'You've got more nerve than any boy I ever knew. First you come and eat our ham and then you send our aunt's address to your father.'

When Stephan had finished Alex looked sternly at Robin.

'You do see nobody must know he is here. Nobody at all, not Mrs O'Brien or, of course, Aunt Dymphna, or people you meet like in the shop or at the sale today.'

Robin got up.

'I don't know why you didn't tell me right away, I'm the only one in this family who is a born sleuth.'

This, when Alex and Penny thought about it, was true. At home for hours together Robin and the other small boys in Royal Crescent, sometimes with bows and arrows, sometimes with knives, sometimes with guns, sleuthed each other or one of the parents. He was experienced at remaining hidden with little or no cover. If anyone was qualified to guard Stephan and spot strangers it was Robin.

Naomi, who had been tucked into her side of the bed by Penny, sat up.

'But what will you use to sleuth with? You haven't got any of your sleuthing things here.'

Stephan made an impatient noise.

'This is children's talk. I do not need the protection of a little boy.'

This annoyed all the Gareths, especially Penny, who was finding herself increasingly motherly about her family.

'We're not interested in what you think. Robin is very good at sleuthing and you're jolly lucky if he offers to help you, which I dare say he won't after you being so rude.'

'I will,' said Robin, 'though if you want to know I think you're a horrid boy.'

Alex got up and nudged Stephan with one foot.

'Get back to your room. Now we all know about you it will be easier to bring you food, which is more than you deserve.'

'Perhaps I do not wish to go to bed yet,' said Stephan.

Alex gave him a little kick.

'There's a quick answer to that. Get up and march or there'll be no breakfast for you tomorrow.'

While they undressed Robin for once in his life was quiet, which was so unusual that Alex asked why.

'Are you planning how best to guard Stephan?'

Robin hopped into bed.

'No. In a place like this that's easy. It's him. I'm sure I've seen him before.'

'Of course you have, on the aeroplane wearing black glasses, he was the boy who was sick, and he was at Cork aerodrome still wearing glases.'

Robin shook his head.

'It's difficult with only candles to see by but it wasn't then, it was somewhere else. I'll look carefully in the morning but I bet I'm right. I know – I absolutely know I've seen him before.'

18

The Sun Shines

THE next morning was gloriously fine. The hills, which in Ireland the children discovered, were a mysterious blue-purple, made a splendid background to emerald green fields, patches of brown bog and the blue, blue sea frothing round rocks covered with golden seaweed.

The first up was Penny and she hung out of the window feeling sort of giddy with so much loveliness all at once. Then she saw Aunt Dymphna. She was pushing the wheelbarrow she had bought at the sale across the field, between the shrubs and rhododendrons which marked what she called 'my drive'. Suddenly there were shrill, sad cries and out of the sky flew what looked to Penny about fifty seagulls wheeling and crying, very white, golden-beaked and beautiful against the blue of the sky.

Aunt Dymphna was dressed in what seemed to be her morning clothes, that is, her usual black cape and man's check hat and Wellingtons, but over her black dress the red and black apron. She put down the wheelbarrow and lifted her arms to the birds, who flew down and sat on them as well as on her shoulders and her hat. Like that she looked like a giant bird talking to tiny birds.

'And she is talking,' Penny thought. 'Except that I don't believe a person can talk to seagulls.'

Aunt Dymphna tilted back her head, which made five seagulls lose their footing on her hat. She raised her wrinkled old face to the sky so that the sun shone on it.

'Now she looks more as if she was praying for something, or perhaps saying "thank you",' thought Penny. 'I wish I believed she could talk to seagulls, I'd run down and ask her what they say about Daddy, but I don't so I can't.'

Naomi, who woke at that moment, had no such inhibitions, she joined Penny at the window, then opened it and leant out.

'Are they telling you about Daddy?'

With a swirl of white wings and a cascade of mewing the seagulls flashed back into the sky and were gone.

Aunt Dymphna shook a fist at Naomi.

'Foolish child! Never interfere when friends are talking privately. You drove them away. They are shy, you know, but they were about to tell me something, indeed they tell me everything.'

Penny surprised herself.

'Suppose they had said anything do you think it was good news?'

Aunt Dymphna looked up at her, there was a half smile round her mouth.

'If you knew seagulls as I know them you would have been able to feel they had something good to say.'

Aunt Dymphna pushed the barrow round the side of the house. Naomi clasped her hands.

'Oh, Penny, perhaps Daddy is better and is coming home.'

'It's silly to believe in seagull news,' said Penny, 'and I'm not going to, but perhaps we'll get a cable today. I think there's sure to be one.'

Naomi was putting on her dressing-gown; now she stopped, a stricken look on her face.

'Penny Gareth, did you hear what Aunt Dymphna said? She said her seagulls told her everything. Just suppose that's true, they'll tell her about Stephan.'

The thought of Stephan made the day less beautiful for Penny.

'I don't believe her seagulls tell her anything, she just imagines it, poor old thing, it's only when the seagulls are there you can't help wondering. Run along and wash. I suppose Stephan will have to have an egg for breakfast and I grudge cooking him anything.'

It made life a lot easier now that Robin and Naomi knew, for Penny sent them up with his breakfast, Robin carrying the tray and Naomi the cup of tea so it wouldn't splash into the saucer.

Stephan was still in bed. He sat up when Robin and Naomi came in. His first look was at the tray.

'Why is it all eggs are boiled?' he said 'I like mine *en cocotte*.'

Neither Robin nor Naomi knew what that meant, but they knew what they thought about a fugitive who was ungrateful and could not even say 'good morning'.

'We don't know what sort of egg that is,' said Naomi, 'but it's very kind of our sister Penny to cook for you at all.'

Stephan's face took on the sulky expression Alex and Penny had come to know all too well.

'You are all horrible to me. It is not my fault I am a refugee, you should have pity, it is not nice for me here.'

Robin glared at Stephan.

'This room was supposed to be nice enough for Naomi, so it's more than nice enough for you.'

Stephan looked sulkier than ever. He had enormous blue eyes that turned nearly black when he was cross.

'How do you dare to speak to me like that, little boy?'

Robin, who had been working out plans for protecting Stephan, was furious.

'Little boy! If you talk like that I'll go round the place shouting, "We've got a boy hiding in our house."'

That frightened Stephan.

'You wouldn't do that, Robin. You promised you wouldn't talk.'

Naomi, who was hungry, moved to the door.

'Come on, Robin. Let's have breakfast, it's no good talking to him,' and she clattered off down the back stairs.

Robin tried to remember the right way to talk to suspicious characters. He spoke out of the side of his mouth.

'Don't worry, I won't split, but you are rumbled, Stephan, so watch out.'

'Well?' Alex asked when Robin took his place at the kitchen table. 'Did you recognize him by daylight?'

'How do you mean?' asked Penny. 'We all saw him on the aeroplane and at the airport.'

Alex helped himself to bread.

'Robin said last night he'd seen him somewhere else.'

Naomi dropped her egg-spoon.

'So have I! I was wondering and wondering why I thought I knew him.'

Alex was sure Robin and Naomi were imagining things, so he said dismissingly:

'Oh, well, I dare say it will come back to you.'

Robin felt aggrieved.

'All right, don't believe me, but you'll be sorry for there's something else I noticed which I was going to tell you and now I won't.'

Penny decided it was time to change the subject.

'As it's such a glorious day, would you like to have a picnic? We could take our bathing things.'

In a second Stephan was forgotten.

'What will we eat at a picnic?' Robin asked.

'Could we buy something at the shop?' Naomi suggested.

'I'll take a prawning net just in case,' said Alex. 'If I can find some string I could mend the net on the beach.'

There is much more to having a picnic, Penny discovered, than just going. There was tidying their rooms, which had to be done first. This meant a near quarrel with Alex and Robin, who had not made their beds since they arrived but had merely pulled the sheets and blankets up. But yesterday she had helped Stephan make their beds properly and she had no intention of making a habit of doing it.

'Make them properly and put the room tidy; because the house is pretty awful it makes it worse if you don't try.'

'You're getting more bossy every day,' growled Alex. 'If Robin and I don't mind if our beds are made properly what's it got to do with you?'

'Don't be mean,' said Penny. 'It's not that I'm bossy but somebody has to try and I seem to be the only one to do it.'

Robin was in two minds about going on the picnic.

'Don't you think I ought to snoop around here?' he asked Alex. 'Anybody could get in while we're all out.'

Alex remembered the days when he had played cops and robbers he had never been an enthusiastic sleuth like Robin, but keen enough to know Robin had to be taken seriously.

'I'm certain nobody knows Stephan is here at the moment. The dangerous time will be when his father tries to join up with him. Then we really will have to watch out. If you could snoop about round the shop and find out if anyone has seen strangers in the neighbourhood it would help.'

Robin liked the sound of that.

'Good. I'll be a sort of counter-spy – you know, on both sides.'

'But you mustn't breathe a word remember.'

'I do think somebody ought to tell Aunt Dymphna about the picnic,' Penny said, 'because I rather think she thinks we're going to garden. I'm afraid it ought to be you to tell her, Alex.'

Alex knew Penny was right so, though unwilling, he went to Aunt Dymphna's side of the house; he found her in her dining-room crouched over a very old torn seed catalogue.

'Good morning, dear boy,' she said. 'Splendid reading this. Herbs – I will have a herb garden.'

'If it's all right with you we were going to have a picnic on the beach.'

'Splendid! Splendid! Bring me back some prawns, admirable eating.'

Alex did not want to look a fool but if Aunt Dymphna was expecting prawns she ought to be warned how little he knew.

'We've never stayed in a place where there are prawns, can you catch them anywhere?'

Aunt Dymphna did not look up from her catalogue.

'They sought it with thimbles, they sought it with care;
     They pursued it with forks and hope;
They threatened its life with a railway-share;
     They charmed it with smiles and soap.'

'Silly old thing!' thought Alex. 'That's a fat lot of help.'
Out loud he said: 'But truly, where do I catch them?'

'That comes from "The Hunting of the Snark" by Lewis
Carroll and is very good advice. We will garden tomorrow,
preparing my herb bed."

'Did she want to garden?' Penny asked when Alex came
back to the kitchen.

Alex rummaged in the dresser drawers looking for a piece
of string with which to mend a prawning net.

'Goodness knows what she wants, but she did say we would
garden tomorrow. She gets madder every day. I asked her
where I would get prawns and do you know what she said,
in poetry of course? Look for them with thimbles and
threaten their lives with railway shares. It's absolutely hopeless talking to her about anything.'

Penny, who was cutting bread-and-butter, saw it would be
better to change the subject.

'I thought we'd buy tins of sardines and things in the
shop for sandwiches. Stephan is having hard-boiled eggs
again. I hope he doesn't get ill, he has very odd meals.'

'Fat lot I'd care if he did,' Alex growled. 'What are we
going to have for supper? We'll need something proper after
sardines for dinner.'

'I like the way they all expect me to look after them,'
Penny thought, but instead of it making her low-spirited it
was beginning to make her sort of proud.

'I'll ask Mrs O'Brien on the way to the beach, she's sure
to think of something. Tell the others to hurry, it's such a
simply glorious day I hate to miss a minute of it.'

Alex slammed the drawer shut.

'There's nothing in this house that anybody wants, and
you better watch out or you'll be as mad as Aunt Dymphna,
hark at you raving about the weather like some green-faced
poet!'

19

The Lady on the Beach

IRELAND was so breath-takingly lovely that morning that if it were not for having no news of their father it would have been perfect.

'It's like Aunt Dymphna's and my poetry,' said Naomi.

> 'I will make a palace fit for you and me,
> Of green days in forests and blue days at sea.'

'You be careful or the seagulls will come pecking,' said Robin, but only half-heartedly for if ever there was a blue day at sea this was it.

'If I could be sorry for Stephan I was this morning,' Penny remarked to no one in particular. 'Imagine being all day in that awful bedroom!'

Alex refused to worry about Stephan.

'We said he could walk up and down the passage, what more does he want?'

Robin agreed with Alex.

'And three hard boiled eggs and bread and butter and milk is just as good as we're having.'

'All the same,' said Penny, 'I was glad Mrs O'Brien told me meat was coming for tonight, if he has many more eggs he'll turn into a hen.'

Naomi tried to imitate Mrs O'Brien.

'There will be a fine piece of meat which I will be putting in the oven for yous, yous can have it hot tonight and then cold with potatoes in their jackets for Sunday.'

The other three laughed for Naomi was rather good at imitations, and anyway it was a morning when it was easy to laugh at anything.

Alex had no wish to go to the shop again for he was self-conscious meeting strangers in Ireland; Robin seemed to be able to jabber to them but he felt they were laughing at him.

'I'll take the stuff to the beach,' he said to Penny, 'while you shop.'

'I'm going with Penny,' Robin stated, 'I must make contacts.'

'And so am I,' Naomi said. 'If there's to be cake for the picnic I'd like to help choose it.'

Alex carried all the bathing things and the prawning net on to the beach opposite the shop. Then, using the prawning net as a stick, he clambered over the rocks to look at the sea-birds. They were a fascinating lot but he knew very few of them by sight. 'I wonder,' he thought, 'if Aunt Dymphna has a bird book amongst all those books on her floors.' Then, bobbing about in the water he saw something extraordinary. It was a head, brownish grey and smooth, and the creature – whatever it was – looked at him with what seemed friendly eyes. Alex was thrilled, he had never seen any wild animal like it before. Very quietly he climbed over another rock to get a nearer view. The creature did not seem to mind him, in fact almost he thought it seemed pleased to see him.

'He's enjoying the sun, isn't he?' said a woman's voice.

Alex had thought he was alone so he jumped. Then he saw there was a lady in a boat on the water below the rocks on which he was standing; she was old but not nearly as old as Aunt Dymphna. She was scooping water out of the bottom of the boat and throwing it overboard.

'What is it?' Alex asked.

The lady did not stop bailing.

'A seal. You often see them round here and there are heaps farther down the water.'

Alex stared respectfully at the seal. Of course that was what it was, he had seen them in the London Zoo but he had never expected to meet one free.

'I do hope it stays until the others come.'

'Who are the others?'

'My two sisters and my brother.'

The lady gave Alex a quick look.

'Are you staying at Reenmore?'

'Yes, that's us, with our aunt, well, our great-aunt really.'

'I know her, in fact I lent sheets and blankets when she knew you were coming. How's your father?'

'Holding his own.'

The lady looked at the prawning net.

'Going prawning?'

Alex felt extraordinarily at ease, much more so than he usually did with a stranger.

'Aunt Dymphna said there were prawns and I ought to catch them. She expects me to bring home some for her but when I asked how she just said some rubbish about looking for them with thimbles and threatening their lives with a railway share.'

The lady laughed.

'She would! She's crazy about Lewis Carroll.'

'She's crazy period' said Alex.

'Not crazy, but mad, so mad she's much saner than most of us. A glorious woman your aunt, I adore her. She was quoting from "The Hunting of the Snark." It's "The Barrister's Dream", you know.'

Alex did not know, and his opinion of the lady sank a bit, nobody could be really nice who thought Aunt Dymphna more sane than most people. He looked back at the sea.

'He's still there. I better go back and warn the others so they don't make a noise.'

The lady sloshed some more rainwater out of her boat.

'If you want them to stay sing to them, at least that's what they say hereabouts.'

'Sing to them!' Alex knew he sounded as though he thought everyone in Ireland was mad. So he asked in a more polite voice: 'Sing what?'

'What you guess they would like, of course.'

Alex felt the lady was thinking him what Aunt Dymphna had called him – poor town boy. It was sickening just as they were getting on so well.

'Well, good-bye.'

'If you want prawns go up the road to the top of the hill, turn left and through the gates. The people are away but in the season they've good prawns on their beach, early yet but you might get a few. The tide should be just right in two hours, it's going out.'

Alex clung to what he understood.

'In two hours, thanks awfully. You're sure the people the house belongs to won't mind?'

The lady laughed.

'How can they when they aren't there? You catch prawns – if you catch them – just as the tide turns when it starts to come.'

Alex was doubtful how much of this he understood.

'Thanks awfully. I hope I catch some.'

'You'll want something to put them in. You pass my cottage on the way to the prawns. Anyone will tell you.'

'I'm afraid I don't know your name.'

'It's a white cottage just below the shop. Ask anyone where Miss Oonagh lives, they'll tell you, and if the others would like to prawn too I could lend some nets.'

Alex knew one thing for certain. Afterwards everybody could catch prawns, this first time he must be the only one and no one must watch him trying to catch them. He wanted more than anything he had wanted for ages to be able to say to Aunt Dymphna 'Oh, by the way, here are your prawns.' That would teach the silly old coot he wasn't the idiot she thought he was.

'I think today they have all got things to do, but another time we'll be very grateful.'

The lady looked up and smiled, as though she understood.

'Right. See you later.'

Penny was finding shopping with Robin and Naomi in Ireland as embarrassing as Alex had done. As before the shop was full of people having drinks, and this time there were people shopping as well. The man with the twinkling eyes was there and he greeted Robin and Naomi as old friends.

'How are yous now? Has your aunt been out on her broomstick, and have you found her old black cat?'

'There isn't one,' said Robin. 'Naomi and I have looked everywhere.'

'It's a grand old place, Reenmore,' said another man whom they had also met the last time they were in the shop. 'There could be a regiment of cats and each of them spitting and swearing and you never catching a sight or sound of the one of them.'

A regiment of cats, each spitting and swearing! It was a terrible picture. Naomi gazed in horror at the man who had spoken.

'You don't really think there could be, you're making it up? But you are right, it is a big house where anything could hide ...'

Robin raised his voice to drown Naomi.

'You couldn't hide anything there, he's teasing you, Naomi.' Then he turned to the man. 'We know every corner of the house now, and the outhouse and the garage. Anyway, I should think it would be very difficult to hide anything in these parts, everybody seems to know about everybody else.'

Bernadette-the-shop laughed.

'Hark at him now and the place trod under with the summer visitors!'

Robin could feel that any second now Penny was going to interrupt and start ordering food, so he rushed on.

'But I bet you know where everyone is staying, just as you know we come from Reenmore.'

A red-haired man agreed with him.

'He has the right of it there. There is never a stranger in these parts but we are knowing who he is and where he will be going.' It was all Robin could do not to give Penny and Naomi a triumphant look. How was that for sleuthing?

Penny, who had been standing awkwardly first on one leg and then on the other, hating being one of a family who was the centre of attention, was glad to turn to the subject of food.

'Three tins of sardines and a cake, please, and have you any tins of vegetables? And I want some soap powder to wash clothes.'

Alex came along the road to meet them.

'I say, come as quickly as you can and don't make a sound. I've something simply marvellous to show you.'

The shopping was dumped on the beach and Penny, Robin and Naomi followed Alex over the rocks. When he stopped they all looked where he pointed.

'What is it?' Penny asked in a whisper.

'A seal.'

Robin could not believe his ears.

'How do you know? Seals are zoo things.'

Naomi gave an excited skip.

'A seal! I've seen a seal!'

'Oh, don't go,' Penny pleaded. 'Please stay, seal, we won't hurt you.'

The seal seemed a little restless with so many eyes on him. He turned his head out to sea.

'A lady I saw on the beach,' whispered Alex, 'told me he

was a seal. She said the way to get them to stay was to sing to them.'

'Sing what?' asked Penny.

'She said to sing what seals like.'

'What about something of the Beatles?' Robin suggested. 'Most people like them.'

'But they aren't people,' Penny objected. 'I'd think something quieter.'

'I know what they'd like,' said Naomi, 'because it's about them,' and without explaining she piped up:

'All things bright and beautiful . . .'

At once Robin joined in and, though a little embarrassed, so after a second did Penny and then Alex:

'All creatures great and small.
All things wise and wonderful,
The Lord God made them all.'

Evidently Naomi's choice was good for the seal not only stayed but came farther in.

Four hours later the children, full of sea-salt and sunshine, crawled wearily back to Reenmore, Alex proudly carrying five prawns in a small can lent by Miss Oonagh.

'I bet old Stephan will be glad to hear us come in,' said Robin.

Penny could even be sorry for Stephan.

'Poor beast, it must have been pretty beastly for him! Imagine how he'll feel when he hears we saw a seal!'

'I don't think he's a seal sort of boy,' said Naomi.

'How right you are,' Alex agreed. 'I'd take a bet all he'll say is "In my country we have thousands of seals."'

Penny remembered there had to be supper.

'Oh, how I hope Mrs O'Brien has remembered she promised to put the meat in the oven.'

But it was not Mrs O'Brien who was in the kitchen, it was Aunt Dymphna. She was standing on a chair, half singing and half speaking:

'Where the bee sucks, there suck I:
  In a cowslip's bell I lie;
  There I couch when owls do cry.
  On the bat's back I do fly
  After summer merrily.
Merrily, merrily, shall I live now
Under the blossom that hangs on the bough.

Merrily, merrily, children, look what the creamery van has brought.' She pointed to a cable lying on the table. 'I have known it all day. My seagulls told me.'

The children rushed to the table. Alex got there first. He tore open the cable and read it out loud.

'Daddy has turned the corner he will get well now bless you darlings Mummy.'

Good news can be as upsetting as bad. Penny sank into a chair and cried and cried.

20

Beginning to Grow

THE cable was followed a week later by a letter. In it their mother admitted that when she first reached the hospital she did not think their father had much chance.

'... but he is a great fighter and little by little he is coming back to life. When I sent that cable the doctor in charge had just said: "I believe we can say he is off the danger list." I was so excited I almost danced.'

'It is too early yet,' she wrote, 'to make plans, but what I hope to manage is that I can bring Daddy home just before your school terms begin.'

The last part of the letter, which would have been such frightful news when they first came, was less bad now they were getting used to Reenmore. In fact, knowing they would be staying for weeks gave them all a settling down feeling.

From those first five prawns Alex had become ambitious. One day he brought home nearly fifty, not very big but after giving Aunt Dymphna ten, enough for them all to have some on bread and butter and to donate one each to Stephan.

'But, mind you, I grudge even one,' Robin said. 'I'm giving him my smallest.'

'Miss Oonagh says I can prawn on her bit of beach,' Alex told Penny, 'and I'm hoping that soon she will take me out catching mackerel, that will be a great help with the food.'

Penny was less enthusiastic, prawns were very nice but even just boiling them was work which somehow none of the others understood.

'Once or twice will be all right for mackerel but we shan't want them every day, and I hope Miss Oonagh shows you how to clean them because I won't. Mrs O'Brien says she likes shop fish because what comes in from the sea makes a terrible old mess.'

In the week after the cable arrived the question of a laundry cropped up again for on the kitchen table Penny found clean sheets and pillow cases. A double pair for her bed and single ones for the others. When she gave out the clean sheets she tried to sound as if she had known all along clean ones would turn up.

'Now when you take the dirty ones off,' she instructed the three boys, 'fold up the dirty ones so that they go in a parcel to the laundry.'

Alex and Robin thought Penny was an awful fuss-pot about bed-making but they did as she told them. But Stephan was as disobliging as usual.

'Why must I change the sheets, that is a girl's job?'

Penny was by now used to his nastiness.

'You can go on using the dirty ones if you'd rather. You don't think I'd care.'

Grumbling, Stephan stripped the bed.

'Why are you always so horrible to me?'

'Because you deserve it. Believe me, it's tough enough cooking and cleaning for my own family without having you to think about.'

'You'd be cross,' Stephan whined, 'up here all day long – with nothing to do except when Robin and Naomi come to play.'

Penny looked at him. He certainly had not improved in appearance since he had come to Reenmore. He had a peeky look and was a greenish colour, rather like a hyacinth bulb when it first came out of the dark.

'I tell you what. I'll try and find you something to read. I suppose you can read English, can't you?'

'Naturally.'

'It isn't natural at all for a foreigner. I can't say when for it will have to be a time when our aunt is out, but she's got masses of books in her part of the house, and I should think that there would be something you would like.'

Actually Stephan's life, for all his grumbling, was much better now that Robin and Naomi knew about him for both spent quite a lot of time with him. Robin, not letting

Stephan know, looking upon his visits to him as part of his job as sleuth in chief.

'I'll watch him and watch him,' he told Alex, 'for I'm sure one day I'll remember where I've seen him before, and I'm watching him for something else.'

Alex was not really interested for he had accepted Stephan as a necessary evil and had small hope anyone was tracking him down, more likely they'd have to let him stay until his father turned up. So he paid no attention to Robin's hints, which later on he was to regret.

Naomi found Stephan useful. The games Aunt Dymphna had bought at the sale turned out to be quite good, especially the one called Spillikins. Aunt Dymphna had taught her how to play it. She had piled the little mother-of-pearl sticks into a heap.

'Now here's a hooked piece for you and here's one for me. The game is to pick out one stick without shaking any of the others. Splendid game!'

And it was, but the difficulty was for Naomi to persuade the others to play with her, and the same applied to tiddly-winks, which was inside the Compendium of Games, and to draughts, but Stephan was a captive playfellow. It was no good his saying he had other things to do because clearly he hadn't. They had no table to play on but there was nothing wrong with the floor. So any time that Naomi was not out she could be heard what Alex called 'putting Stephan in his place'.

'You shook that stick, Stephan, and you know you did. You are the most awful cheat.'

'You are stupid at tiddlywinks, it's easy, don't press so hard.'

But when it was draughts Stephan often won, then Naomi would say:

'I'm tired of draughts, you always win. Now we'll play Spillikins again.'

Of course there were worries. Alex could see the end in sight of the twenty-five pounds, going the way it was going it would not last until they went home. One day he would have to tackle Aunt Dymphna about cashing the cheque. He did think about asking his mother in a letter what arrangements she had made about paying for them, but he had decided that she ought not to be worried about anything and he had told this to the others.

'We can all write but just tell her nice things, it's no good fussing her about anything as she's got Daddy to bother about.'

Penny worried about everything because she was a natural worrier. She worried she was feeding the others on wrong food and they would get ill. She worried that the younger ones were not having fun and then, when she and Alex agreed that they might go on the beach alone, she worried they would drown. She even worried about Stephan. How long could you keep a boy indoors without his getting ill? Of course she saw his window was open, but could you get ill from never going outside?

Robin worried about keeping Stephan a secret. He found it terribly hard not to tell Aunt Dymphna, Mrs O'Brien and people in the shop about him. He had once said 'I don't think there should be even a tiny pause in talk, people should talk all the time.' And he still believed this, to him there was meanness in keeping something interesting to himself. It made him ashamed to think how hurt all his friends in the shop would be if they knew he was not telling them about Stephan.

Naomi was not exactly worried about anything but Aunt Dymphna was making her think – something she had never done before. It had started the very day after the cable came. Aunt Dymphna, her coat flying, had rushed into the kitchen where the children were having a late, leisurely breakfast.

'Hurry! Hurry! Hurry! Church is eleven o'clock. In the lane ten-thirty sharp.'

There had been an awful rush for, not knowing they were going to church, they were all dressed in jeans and jerseys, but by leaving the washing up until they got back they all succeeded in getting into the clothes they had travelled in.

But in the rush somebody trod on Naomi's foot and Penny had refused to let her wear a green dress of which she was fond.

'That frock you travelled in is O.K. Do think of me and dirty out one thing before you start on another. I don't see you offering to wash your own things.'

One way and another it was an aggrieved Naomi who got into the car.

'I do think you're mean, Penny,' she mewed. 'I like the green dress and my foot still hurts.'

Alex and Penny tried to quieten her.

'Poor old thing!' Alex commiserated. 'But I'm sure it will stop hurting soon.'

'I'm sorry about the frock, darling,' Penny said, 'but truly washing's awfully hard work.'

'You haven't done any yet,' Naomi persisted, 'so how do you know? Mummy never minds doing it.'

Aunt Dymphna brought the car to one of her dramatic stops.

'Tiffs and tantrums! Grizzles and grouses! If I were your sister or your brothers I would take you out to sea and drown you, Naomi. Ever since you came into my beautiful home I hear your voice raised in moans. Throw her over the hedge, Alex, we do not want her with us.'

Alex had not thrown Naomi over the hedge but the threat had stopped her whines, and for the rest of the drive and during the sermon in church she had thought about what Aunt Dymphna had said. At first her thoughts had been of the 'It's mean. It's mean. I'm only little, I bet she cried sometimes when she was only nine' variety. But presently she began to wonder. Always she had found tears as a last resort were the best way to get what she wanted, and she had certainly used them more than usual since she came to Ireland. Sometimes because she couldn't help it, but quite often because she knew Alex and Penny would give in if she did. Perhaps – just perhaps – she would try to cry a little less. As it happened, on the way back from church, her resolution was put to the test.

'Could we take a picnic tea on the beach, Penny?' she had asked.

Penny remembered what Aunt Dymphna had said to Alex about her herb bed.

'We could unless you want us for your garden, Aunt Dymphna?'

'Certainly today we shall garden. "The child that is born on the Sabbath day is bonny and blithe and good and gay," and the same applies to seeds.'

Naomi was just going to say 'But I want to go on the beach' when she stopped. She didn't intend Aunt Dymphna to say anything more about taking her out to sea and drowning her.

Alex, who knew that only the day before Aunt Dymphna had not got farther than a seed catalogue, was surprised at this talk of gardening.

'Have you got the herb seeds already?'

'No, dear boy. But earth prepared on the Sabbath can also be blithe and gay.' She swerved to avoid a dog and all the family leant out of the windows to shout 'We are going home to Reenmore.' 'So,' Aunt Dymphna continued when the dog had retired, 'today we will garden.'

'When it's done what will you plant?' Penny asked, more to be polite than because she cared. She might have known by then what would happen. Aunt Dymphna, swerving her car backwards and forwards across the road in time to the words, recited:

> 'Excellent herbs had our fathers of old—
>   Excellent herbs to ease their pain—
> Alexanders and Marigold,
>   Eyebright, Orris, and Elecampane,
> Basil, Rocket, Valerian, Rue
>   (Almost singing themselves they run)
> Vervain, Dittany, Call-me-to-you—
>   Cowslip, Melitot, Rose of the Sun.
> Anything green that grew out of the mould
>   Was an excellent herb to our fathers of old.'

When the children were back in the Reenmore kitchen eating cold meat and potatoes in their jackets, Alex said:

'You were an ass, Penny, to ask her what she was going to plant. You might have known she'd find something to spout. And anyway the poor old thing has only got an old catalogue, and whoever heard of half the stuff she mentioned? Rose of the Sun and Elecampane!'

That first Sunday very little was done in the garden to show there would some day be one. In spite of all the rain that had fallen the ground was hard, and it was full of weeds, but after a week's work there was enough dug-up earth to make them think of planting. Then one morning Penny had a great idea. It was the day she had gone over to Aunt Dymphna's side of the house to look for a book for Stephan. She searched in what Aunt Dymphna called her dining-room. She sat on the floor beside a vast dusty pile of books looking for anything that could interest a boy of twelve when exactly what – without knowing it – she wanted for herself fell open in her lap. It was a huge book on cooking and household management written by somebody called Mrs Beeton.

Penny resisted the temptation to read about things to cook and went on with her search. Presently she came across *Ivanhoe*, 'and that will keep him going for ages,' she thought. She was on her way out of the room when she knocked a book off another pile which was just inside the door; it fell open and with a pleased squeak she knelt down beside it and read the title out loud: *The Courtship of Yonghy-Bonghy-Bò* by Edward Lear. So that was how Yonghy-Bonghy-Bò was spelt! Penny shut the book and put it on top of *Ivanhoe* and the cookery book. Then she smiled to herself. She would not give Aunt Dymphna another chance to ask 'Are you a savage, child?' She would learn the poem and give her a surprise. A surprise! It was as she thought of a surprise that her idea came to her. Hugging the three dusty books she ran back to the kitchen where Alex was washing mud off the family's gumboots, which they had worn for gardening.

'I say, I've got a gorgeous idea. You know how keen Aunt Dymphna is to have a herb garden? Well, I bet she's never even written for the seeds. So why don't we buy them and give her a surprise?'

21

Washing

THE weather became beautiful. For whole days the sun streamed down and Ireland looked more and more glorious. Without noticing it the children's lives fell into a pattern. After breakfast at least three times a week they gardened; none of them liked doing it but Aunt Dymphna was not a person to listen to excuses. At the first bird-like flap of her cloak they were pulling on their gumboots, and even Naomi kept what she felt to herself.

Most days after gardening the children picnicked on the beach in spite of daily protests from Stephan.

'You are the most selfish family I have met. How would you wish to be me alone hour after hour eating hard-boiled eggs?'

'Shut up and be thankful you get anything,' Alex growled.

'Mostly hard-boiled eggs is what we have,' said Penny, 'and you always have a good supper.'

Robin thought that was going too far.

'Not always – sometimes it's simply awful but at least you get the same as us.'

'Don't bother with him,' Naomi advised, 'he thinks he's the most important person in the house instead of the least important.'

From the beach they usually went their separate ways. After a bathe, when the tide was right, Alex prawned or sometimes went out with Miss Oonagh in her boat. They had not yet caught any mackerel, but rumour had it some had been caught up the coast so hope was rising.

Penny could not carry the vast Mrs Beeton book to the beach, but it was falling to pieces so every day she was able to bring a different section down with her. The section she knew ought to be the most helpful was the one she avoided

for it stung her conscience. The horrid truth was that in one
of the rooms off the kitchen a shameful pile of washing was
collecting, all their sheets and all their dirty clothes. But
from the quick, unwilling glance Penny had given Mrs
Beeton on washing she was not helpful for those who
wanted to do laundry in Reenmore. 'Fill pans with lukewarm
water,' Mrs Beeton advised, 'and let the clothes soak over-
night.' What pans? And in what water? What would Mrs
Beeton advise when your water was brown with peat and old
leaves? Mrs Beeton gave the most wonderful advice on
managing servants, but none at all about how you managed
to do laundry in a house that had not, as far as could be discovered, clean water or an iron.

Robin had made friends amongst the local boys for school
had broken up and the scholars, as he discovered school-
children were called in Ireland, were willing to allow him to
join in their games.

'They think I'm just one of them,' Robin told Alex, 'they

don't know I'm joining because I'm sleuthing. They're very useful because they know everything that's going on, so no stranger could hang about here without them noticing.'

Actually, though it was true he was sleuthing, Robin had a very good time with the local boys, helping with the farm animals, or collecting winkles from the beach when the tide was low. This last was also a source of income, for when a sack was full it was placed on the side of the road to be picked up later by a lorry. Someone – Robin never discovered who – paid ten shillings for each sack, for winkles were exported all over Europe, and usually when the money arrived for the winkles the odd shilling would be given to Robin for his help.

Naomi made friends with the local girls and she too sometimes helped to gather winkles, but mostly she was being taught Irish reels which the girls learned in schools, and unconsciously they also taught her to speak like themselves, so that when she was with them Naomi sounded like a native. They were tough, resourceful children in West Cork, expecting to look after themselves and make their own amusements, so Naomi had to be constantly on her guard to see that she lived up to their standards.

Then one morning Penny woke up early. She was leaning out of her bedroom window when she saw Aunt Dymphna hurrying across the field carrying wet sheets. These she hung on the fuchsia hedge to dry.

'So she washes hers herself,' thought Penny. 'But where does she wash them and what in?'

When Aunt Dymphna was back in the house Penny, in gumboots and a dressing-gown, nipped out of the front door and ran across the field. Her worst fears were realized. You could not wash things in cold rainwater and get them clean. Aunt Dymphna's sheets were brownish coloured, just like the rainwater. There were even dead leaves sticking to them. They might look better when they were ironed but Penny doubted it, and anyway where was there an iron? While Penny was examining the sheets Aunt Dymphna appeared in her usual sudden way standing beside her.

'Good morning, dear. Such an obliging plant fuchsia. It never grumbles however much laundry I load on to it.'

'Where do you keep the iron?' Penny asked. 'I've never seen one.'

'Iron! What do you want an iron for? Sun and wind are all damp linen requires.'

'Are they? I thought sheets had to be ironed.'

It was a blustery morning. Aunt Dymphna pranced up and down, her cloak flying.

> 'Gold is for the mistress – silver for the maid!
> Copper for the craftsman cunning at his trade.
> "Good!" said the Baron, sitting in his hall,
> But Iron – Cold Iron – is master of them all.'

Penny was irritated. Aunt Dymphna had only one pair of sheets to wash, she had four pairs, one of them double – and pillow cases and clothes. Why couldn't she be helpful just once instead of spouting poetry?

She could not think of anything to say that was not rude so she turned to go, but Aunt Dymphna made one of her bird-like swoops and caught her by the wrist.

'You worry too much, child. Whenever I see you there is an anxious frown on your face or you are looking at your watch. What for, I should like to know? You are in Ireland, child, and here they have never accepted time, they refuse to know him, and very sensible too, none of us should know him.'

Penny thought of her hungry family demanding food at one o'clock and supper at seven; it was all right for Aunt Dymphna who, if she ate at all, just ate when she was hungry.

'We always do things by time at home so it's difficult to give it up all at once.'

'Of course it is, but you'll learn, dear child, and today I'm going to pamper you, I'm going to give you some time.' She caught hold of Penny's hand. 'Come along. Run! Run!'

Panting they arrived at the front door, Penny out of breath.

'My goodness, you do run fast!'

Aunt Dymphna dropped Penny's hand.

'I had to if I was to give you a minute. Now I've given it to you so see you use it carefully.'

Penny stumped crossly down the hall to the kitchen. She opened the door of the room where the dirty laundry was lying and peered at it.

'Silly old thing!' she thought. 'Surely asking for an iron is a very ordinary thing to do. Oh, my goodness, I wish she was more ordinary. Why must my only aunt be so odd?'

It was desperation that made Penny, after she had cleared away the picnic lunch, leave the beach and find Miss Oonagh's cottage. The door backed on to the road, there seemed to be no bell so she knocked.

'There's no sort of use in knocking. First because I'm on the same side of the door as you are.'

Penny jumped.

'Oh, goodness! I thought for a second you were Aunt Dymphna. She's always saying things like that.'

'No, I'm Oonagh and you must be Penny. Come in. You must admit no one could resist quoting the frog-footman when they actually were on the same side of the door as the knocker.'

Penny liked the look of Oonagh so she started straight away on her troubles.

'And it's not just that I don't want to wash them,' she explained when she had told about the sheets, 'but Alex said you said they were yours and truly, washed in our water they'd be spoilt, Aunt Dymphna's are absolutely brown.'

Oonagh had laughed so much at Penny's description of her talk with Aunt Dymphna that tears poured down her cheeks.

'I do feel mean laughing but you describe it so well and you're looking so despairing.'

Penny was almost smiling for Miss Oonagh's laugh was infectious.

'If only sometimes she would tell me things. You know she expects me to cook and I never have.'

Miss Oonagh nodded.

'But I hear from Alex you manage pretty well as a rule.'

'I burnt a chicken up the other day, it was pitch black, nobody could eat it. We had boiled eggs instead and really we eat too many of those.'

Miss Oonagh got up and went to one of her bookshelves; her room was full of books.

'Did you say your aunt quoted something about cold iron?'

'That's right, it's the only bit I remember.'

'I think it's Kipling. *Rewards and Fairies*.' She took a little red book from the shelf. 'Yes, here it is.' Oonagh passed her the book. 'It comes after a story called "Cold Iron". You can borrow it if you like.'

Penny did not want the book, she wanted help, but it was rude not to take it. Politely she glanced through it and then she gave a gasp.

'Oh, that's where the poetry about herbs comes from.'

Oonagh leant over the back of the chair on which Penny was sitting.

'"Our Fathers of Old." A splendid poem. Kipling has been very neglected lately but he's due for a revival, don't you think?'

Penny barely knew the name of Kipling, and had never thought about any poet, but she was flattered that Oonagh should ask her opinion; to be treated as a knowledgeable person made a nice change from the way Aunt Dymphna treated her.

'I expect he is. Aunt Dymphna said all this first verse to us. She's going to have a herb garden. We thought if ever we went to Bantry we could order her some herbs.'

Miss Oonagh shook her head.

'If you think you can just order Eyebright, Orris and Elecampane in a Bantry shop – or indeed any shop – you've got a disappointment coming. You must order them from a nursery. I've got a catalogue somewhere.' She went to her desk and rummaged among the papers.

Penny was afraid Oonagh might forget a dull thing like washing if she got too interested in herbs.

'What would you do if you were me about the washing?'

Oonagh found the catalogue.

'The sheets are easy, I'll ask your aunt to let me have them, I'll say I like them washed here, I'll never dare tell her I'm sending them to a laundry. About the clothes, ask Mrs O'Brien for an extra bucket or two of her well water and a bucket to boil water in. I expect your clothes are nylon which doesn't need ironing. Ah, here's the list of herbs. Chervil, Chives, Lemon Balm, Lovage, Marjoram, Mint, Parsley, Rosemary, Sage, Tarragon and Thyme.'

'Can I borrow the catalogue?'

'You can but I don't think your aunt will want plants of most of these because they grow wild, and she has a theory they should be collected at moonlight when the moon's full.'

'Goodness, has she? She didn't say so.'

'She will, and I expect want you all to help her pick them.'

Penny was horrified.

'Oh, dear, I do hope not! I'd be no good at finding herbs at midnight.'

'Nor me.' Oonagh got up. 'Let's have a cup of tea. And cheer up, you'll find the washing looks much less worrying after I have taken the sheets.'

Even the knowledge that the sheets were going was cheering. Penny came home in a much happier mood. But it was no good, she discovered, pushing your worries aside at Reenmore for something new was sure to crop up.

There was a good supper that night of roast beef which, with the help of Mrs O'Brien, was well cooked and even Stephan said it was good. This was followed by plum pie made by Mrs O'Brien. Covered in thick cream it was food for the gods, so the children were lingering over the last mouthfuls when the kitchen door was flung open and Aunt Dymphna, holding a wicker lobster pot, flew in.

'Just the night to catch a lobster. Come along. Come along, we are going to sea.'

'I didn't know you had a boat,' said Alex.

'I haven't, dear boy, I haven't. But a friend has a row-boat which on occasion he will lend. He is extraordinarily distrustful of my powers and will only lend me the boat when the sea is calm. Today it is calm so away we go.'

Aunt Dymphna looked so pleased and excited that it seemed mean not to be equally enthusiastic. But, as Penny was learning fast, a housewife's work was never done, a hot meal meant a lot of washing up. She certainly couldn't go out looking for lobsters, and she was not going to let Naomi go. But Penny need not have worried. Alex and Robin were as enthusiastic as Aunt Dymphna. They had both jumped up and were dragging on gumboots and jerseys – which as usual they had scattered about the kitchen – before she had finished speaking.

'I've never seen a lobster except in a shop,' said Robin.

Alex did just remember he was in charge.

'Will you be all right, Penny? I mean, with the washing up and everything?'

'I'll dry,' said Naomi. 'As a matter of fact us women get on better with you men out of the way.'

Aunt Dymphna turned to swoop out of the door.

'To sea! To sea! Ahoy! Ahoy, off to sea we go.'

'Can I carry the pot?' Robin asked.

Aunt Dymphna passed it to him.

'Yes, dear boy, yes.

" 'Tis the voice of the Lobster; I heard him declare,
    You have baked me too brown, I must sugar my hair." '

Aunt Dymphna and the boys disappeared up the passage to the front door. Penny and Naomi heard Alex ask what they used for bait, but they did not hear Aunt Dymphna's answer. Then they heard the front door slam and suddenly the house felt very large and very empty.

Penny tried to sound casual.

'I suppose I had better lock the back door.'

'Couldn't we lock the front door too?' Naomi suggested. 'We could open it again before we go to bed.'

22

Adventure

AUNT Dymphna's friend had left his boat ready for her. He had brought her in from where she was moored and had pulled her up the beach. The oars were in the boat and row-locks in place, all that needed doing was to push her into the sea.

'I shall steer,' said Aunt Dymphna, 'for I know where we are going, which is more than you do.'

Lying in the bottom of the boat was some rope, a piece of newspaper with a smelly piece of fish in it and some flat stones.

Robin peered at the fish.

'Is that the bait?' he asked, settling down next to Aunt Dymphna.

'It is, dear boy. It is. A splendid piece of pollock, I believe. Nothing delights a lobster more than pollock.'

Robin looked at the pot.

'Where do you put bait in a lobster pot?'

'Tie it,' said Aunt Dymphna. 'There are strings for the purpose. You can tie the bait, Robin, and you can row, Alex. You do row, I suppose?'

The children had been on the Serpentine when they were smaller, and had been allowed to help with the oars. It had seemed quite easy then.

'Sort of.'

'Good. Then off we go.'

Luckily the sea was dead calm so, though Alex caught a crab or two and had great difficulty in making both oars move at the same time, they moved along, though slowly. But rowing badly is very hard work and soon Alex's arms were aching unbearably.

'The tide is with us,' said Aunt Dymphna. 'Reserve your strength, dear boy, it will be harder rowing home.'

This piece of bad news made Alex notice that it was not only his arms that were aching, it was all of him.

'Get on with fixing that bait,' he told Robin, 'then you can take an oar.'

'It is about fixed I think,' said Robin. He showed Aunt Dymphna the pot. 'Is that all right?'

Aunt Dymphna did not glance at the pot.

'We shall know that if and when we catch a lobster, shan't we? What you need, Alex, is music. Nothing like rhythm,' She raised her head to the stars. Her old cracked voice rang out, matching the creaking of the oars. '"The Owl and the Pussy-cat went to sea...!"'

Alex whispered to Robin.

'Move over and take an oar. I can't row alone much longer.'

Robin, knowing nothing of boats, stood up to move to the seat in front of Alex. Changing places in a boat is always a manoeuvre that needs caution but particularly so when the one who rows is liable to catch a crab. This Alex, watching Robin, promptly did and so tipped Robin into the sea.

'"With a ring on the end of his nose, His nose,"' sang Aunt Dymphna. 'Push out an oar, Alex, and haul him in.'

Getting someone on board a small boat at sea is very difficult. Robin was quite safe for he could swim and anyway had hold of an oar, but though Alex pulled him alongside and held his arms he could not get him into the boat and it tipped to a dangerous angle.

'I think we'll have to tow him to rocks or something,' Alex gasped.

Aunt Dymphna finished her song: '"They danced by the light of the moon, The moon, They danced by the light of the moon." Always finish what you are doing before starting on something new. Now what is the trouble?'

Alex tried not to sound fussed but he did not succeed.

'Robin's in the water and I can't get him back into the boat. I should think he'd catch pneumonia.'

'Not in August, dear boy, not in August.' Aunt Dymphna stood up. 'Now let me see, there should be an island hereabouts.'

'Oh, do sit down,' Alex shouted. 'It's bad enough Robin being in the water without you falling in too.'

Aunt Dymphna sat.

'Don't get so excited,' she said. 'I can feel an island. Row.'

It was as Aunt Dymphna said 'row' that Alex noticed that Robin being in the water was not their only trouble. Evidently, having pulled Robin alongside on an oar, he had not put the oar back in its rowlock and it must have floated away.

He sounded as desperate as he felt.

'I've lost an oar.'

Nothing seemed to worry Aunt Dymphna.

'"They went to sea in a Sieve, they did. In a Sieve they went to sea:"' She leant over the side of the boat. 'Robin, dear boy, I am putting the weights in our lobster pot and attaching the necessary rope and marker. When I see a suitable spot I shall pass the pot to you for you are admirably placed to sink it. But keep hold of the rope, dear boy, or we may lose you. You can't row with one oar, Alex, so we must hope the tide will take us where we wish to go.'

Back at Reenmore Penny and Naomi had finished the washing up.

'I suppose I must unlock the front door now,' said Penny. 'We might go to sleep and not hear them come back. You go up and get started.'

Naomi was quite clear about that.

'No, thank you. Whatever we do we'll do together. While I was putting away the plates in the kitchen I kept expecting a face at the window like Alex saw when it was Aunt Dymphna.'

Penny agreed entirely about their doing things together. It was getting dark and nobody could like Reenmore when it was empty after dark. Hand in hand the girls went to the front door and unlocked it, then hand in hand they climbed the back stairs.

'I suppose we ought to just say good night to Stephan,' said Penny.

'I don't mind tonight,' Naomi agreed, 'because he's sort of company while the boys are out.'

Stephan had not yet gone to bed. He had lit his candle and was reading *Ivanhoe*. He scowled at the girls.

'You did not come to take my plate with the pudding or to ask if I wish for any more.'

'There was no point,' said Naomi. 'There wasn't any more, all there was we ate.'

Stephan closed his book.

'You do not care if I starve.'

'Not much,' Penny agreed. 'We'll take the plate when we bring your breakfast.'

'You will put it outside the door,' Stephan ordered. 'I do not like a dirty plate in my room.'

Penny was always glad to say 'no' to Stephan.

'We can't put it outside tonight, the boys are out and they might fall over it when they come in.'

'Where are they out?'

Naomi was half-way to the door.

'It's not your business but they are catching a lobster with our aunt. Good night.'

In the bedroom Penny and Naomi undressed quickly. They had lit a candle but it did not help much in the dark, shadowy room. Penny saw Naomi's eyes peering into corners.

'It's all right, darling. After all, you are sharing my bed and I should think the others will be back soon.'

'Just in case,' said Naomi, 'do you think it would be cowardly to put our suitcases against the door?'

'They wouldn't be much good as they are empty.'

'I think they'd make me feel better,' Naomi explained.

Penny could see the point.

'All right, we'll put the big one at the bottom, but I hope the boys don't try to come in to say good night.'

Hours later the girls were woken by a shattering clatter. Their doors had been pushed open and the suitcases had toppled to the floor. In the doorway, holding his candle in a shaking hand, was Stephan.

'There is somebody in our field.'

Even half asleep Naomi was not having that.

'You can't say "our" field, it's nothing to do with you.'

Penny put on her dressing-gown.

'It's probably the boys coming back, what time is it?'

'Three o'clock and they are not back, I look to see.'

Not back! Penny felt sick. Out in a boat with Aunt Dymphna – mad, crazy Aunt Dymphna – and not back at three in the morning! She should never have let them go or they should all have gone. Suppose the boys were drowned.

'Not back! I must get help.'

Stephan came to the bed, they could hear his teeth chattering.

'Stop worrying about the boys. There is somebody in the field and it's not them. It's a man.'

'A man!' Naomi scrambled out of bed. 'How do you know? You couldn't see him, it's dark.'

'Something woke me. I went to the window and saw him. He's big and he's carrying a torch or a lantern.'

'Listen!' said Penny. 'Listen!'

They listened. Someone was knocking on the front door.

'And it's not locked,' Naomi moaned.

Stephan clutched at Penny.

'Don't answer. It's someone come for me, I know it is.'

Penny shook him off.

'Don't be so selfish, I hope it's somebody about the boys.' She moved to the window. 'I'll shout and see what it is the man wants.'

Stephan gave a howl.

'You mustn't talk to him. You mustn't. I won't go back. You don't know how awful it is.' He gripped Penny round the waist. 'I won't let you talk to him.'

Naomi was not having that, she got on the floor and crawled towards Stephan.

'Of course she must talk to him if it's about the boys. Let her go.' She gave one of his ankles a sharp bite. She said later she had never enjoyed a bite more.

Stephan gave another howl, this time of pain, and let go of Penny, who ran to the window and flung it open at the bottom.

'Hallo!' she called out. 'Hallo! Is anybody there?'

There was not much moon that night but by its light Penny saw a tall dark shadow detach itself from the other shadows. Then a voice answered but in a language of which she did not understand a solitary word.

She looked over her shoulder.

'I think it must be about you, Stephan, for I think he's talking your language.'

Naomi had joined Penny at the window.

'He isn't. It's the way they talk here. Let me talk to him.'

What seemed to Penny an interminable conversation went on between Naomi and the man, then Naomi left the window. She spoke in a whisper.

'I think he's one of those people Aunt Dymphna calls tinkers. You know, gipsies. He wants something from Aunt Dymphna. I couldn't understand exactly, but I think it's her sort of medicine, the sort she picks. I think somebody's ill.'

'Did you tell him we couldn't do anything, that Aunt Dymphna's out?'

'No, I didn't want him to know there was only us here.'

'I think we ought to get Mrs O'Brien,' said Penny. 'She'll know what to do about that man, and what we should do about the boys and Aunt Dymphna.'

'What could we do about them?'

'I suppose there's a lifeboat would look for them.' Penny tried to remember things she had read. 'I think somebody sends off a rocket. But how can we get out of the front door without that man seeing us?'

Mary and Sheila O'Brien were much older than Naomi so they never played with her and her friends but they were, it was said locally, 'rare leapers' when it came to Irish dancing. So often when Naomi was around she would be given a lesson in the red-tiled kitchen, and naturally the girls had talked to her.

'There's a way to the cottage from the garden at the back,' she told Penny.

'Aunt Dymphna said there wasn't.'

'That's what Aunt Dymphna thinks and no one has ever told her that there is.' Naomi quoted in a fair imitation of the O'Briens, ' "for fear the old one would be popping up and down with never a word to warn you, the way she has", but there is a way down, it's by a rope the same as coming up, and I know where it is. If you keep talking to the man so he thinks we're still here I could fetch Mrs O'Brien.'

Penny was so sick with worry about the boys she had little room for any other sensation, but this was unbelievable.

'You don't mean you'd go alone?'

Never afterwards did Naomi know how she made such an answer:

'Yes, I will.' There was a wobble in her voice which she tried to hide. 'Who's afraid of the big bad wolf?'

23

In the Dead of Night

To country people there is nothing to walking down a back garden at night but to Naomi it was a terrifying experience. Things creaked, shadows moved, birds cried. It was not as if it was a real garden, there was no proper path, only a rough track. Naomi kept losing it and finding herself tripping over half-dug beds. To make it more frightening she could not stop remembering what Aunt Dymphna had said about fairies. It was the day she had said there were no such things as fairies and Aunt Dymphna had answered: 'Quiet, child, quiet. It is safe perhaps to say such things in England but never in Ireland, this is their home.' Was it true? Were there fairies in Ireland and, if there were, what were they like? Was it in Ireland that they stole children?

It was as Naomi was thinking this that something or someone caught hold of her dressing-gown cord. She stood still, cold water collecting on her neck and trickling down her back. Nothing moved, there was no sound; who was holding her? Naomi gave her dressing-gown cord a gentle pull but it was firmly held. Tears ran down her cheeks. Then in a whisper she began to plead.

'I don't know much about fairies but Aunt Dymphna says you live here. Please, please let me go. You see, my brothers are out in a boat, they ought to have been home hours ago and they aren't.' Then, because she was unused to talking to fairies, Naomi finished as if she was saying her prayers: 'and God bless everybody and make me good. Amen.'

Perhaps Naomi moved but something gave a rusty squeak. Only too well Naomi knew that sound. She gave her cord a jerk and it was free. She was still crying but angry with herself.

'Silly me! Fancy not remembering that awful wheelbarrow was there, I suppose my cord caught on the handle.'

It was not easy to scramble down to the O'Briens' yard by the rope in the daytime, for it was fastened to the well. In the dark it meant a lot of groping and the danger of sliding down the bank with a nasty drop on to cobbles. But presently Naomi, on hands and knees, found its rough surface, gripped the rope in both hands and slid. Then she was knocking on the O'Briens' door.

Back at the house Penny was having an idiotic conversation with the man, for he did not understand one word she said and she did not understand anything he said, but in spite of being so worried about the boys she had a feeling the man below was equally worried about something and wanted help desperately. Oh, if only Mrs O'Brien would come!

The O'Briens were heavy sleepers and it was some while before Mrs O'Brien woke up. Then she opened a window and looked out.

'What is it now?'

'It's me,' Naomi explained. 'There's a man up at the house, I think he's a tinker, he wants Aunt Dymphna but she went out with the boys to catch a lobster and they're not back and Penny and I are afraid they're drowned.'

Mrs O'Brien made a clicking noise with her tongue.

'Don't be fretting yourself, it will be a strange day when an accident befalls the old lady, more lives she has than a dozen cats. Is it a tinker now up at the house?'

'I think so but I don't properly understand what he wants. Could you come, please, and talk to him?'

'I could so. Mr O'Brien is away this night with animals for the fair or he would help yous. Wait now, I'll be down as soon as I've drawn on me coat.'

Mrs O'Brien was as good as her word and soon she and Naomi were hurrying up the lane to the house.

'We will not use the old rope in the dark of the night,' said Mrs O'Brien. 'There is too much we might be falling over.'

'Oughtn't we to tell the lifeboat that Aunt Dymphna and
the boys haven't come back?'

'Lifeboat!' Mrs O'Brien gasped. 'And never the sight or
sound of such a thing in these parts. We could be asking
Miss Oonagh, and she having a boat with a motor to drive it.
She went out two winters back when a man was drowned.
They say she had wonderful skill in handling the corpse.'

'Oh, don't!' said Naomi.

'Hush now. There is no danger for Miss Gareth and the
boys, they will be home safe and sound demanding their
breakfast before it is light.'

The tinker was still on the lawn trying to make Penny
understand him. Mrs O'Brien immediately took charge and
a flood of talk poured from the man. Presently Mrs O'Brien
called up to Penny.

'It is a sickness his wife has, she has had it before and the
old lady has the cure for it. Have you seen any bottles of
medicine in the house?'

'Only those old dried leaves in the kitchen. Could they be
medicine?' Penny asked.

'No, those are for cooking, she says they give a wonderful
taste to the food, I have not had a fancy for them myself.'

'I should think we had better wait for Aunt Dymphna,'
Penny said. 'It would be awful if we gave him the wrong
medicine.'

Mrs O'Brien had a long talk with the tinker which apparently satisfied him, for it finished with 'good-bye now' and
he ambled off into the night. Mrs O'Brien refused to get excited about the non-appearance of Aunt Dymphna and the
boys. She repeated her statement about Aunt Dymphna
having more lives than a cat. Placidly she made a pot of tea
while she ruminated on what might be happening at what
she called 'below'.

'Everyone will be knowing the old lady and the boys went
out with the pot for a lobster. There is not enough wind
blowing to ripple the water so what harm could be coming to
them? The old lady can swim and so can the boys, wonderful in the water, they are, I was hearing. There is nothing can

be done before it is light then perhaps, if they have not come home, Miss Oonagh will take out her boat, which has a fine speed to it.'

'Mr O'Brien is away tonight with animals for the fair,' Naomi explained to Penny, 'so there's no one but us to tell Miss Oonagh.'

Penny thought anything – even walking about the lonely countryside in the dark – would be better than staying in the house doing nothing. She was faintly cheered by Mrs O'Brien's calm certainty that nothing was wrong, but she knew she would be gnawed by worry until she saw the boys were alive and well. She put down her cup and got up.

'Come on, Naomi, we better be going.'

Mrs O'Brien thought that foolish.

'There is no need for you to be rushing out into the night, wait until the light comes and like enough the old lady and the boys will be speeding up the hill.'

Penny refused to listen.

'I'd feel happier if we go now.'

Mrs O'Brien collected the dirty cups.

'Will you not be scared now? It is terrible dark on the road and there is no saying what you might be meeting.'

Naomi shivered.

'Why don't we wait until the light, Penny?'

But Penny was firm.

'No, we'll go now. Come up and get some clothes on.'

Stephan, who was still shivering with fright because of the tinker, grew quite hysterical when he heard he was to stay alone in Reenmore.

'And we have to leave the front door open,' said Penny, 'in case the others get back.'

'But what about me?' moaned Stephan. 'Suppose anyone gets in, what am I to do?'

'Keep quiet,' Penny ordered. 'No one knows you are here so they won't look for you.'

Stephan's teeth were chattering.

'This is such a big house. How would you like to be in it alone? As it's dark couldn't I come with you?'

'You really are silly,' said Naomi. 'What shall we do with you when it gets light?'

Penny had no time for Stephan.

'Anyway we're off now, so stop grumbling and go to bed.'

'If I ever could be sorry for Stephan I am now,' Naomi whispered as she and Penny went downstairs. 'I'd simply hate to be left alone here, wouldn't you?'

'Yes, but it would be silly to mind. No one will come to the house and it will soon be light.'

Naomi found it was much easier to be brave when you had company. It was terribly dark on the road and their feet sounded dreadfully noisy, but because Penny was there it was not terrifying like walking through the back garden. They did not talk much and when they did only in whispers for, like their feet, their voices sounded so loud in the night.

'I wish Mrs O'Brien hadn't said that about what you might be meeting,' Penny whispered.

'You know what I was thinking about?' Naomi answered. 'It was in that bit of poetry Alex said Aunt Dymphna told him about crispy pancakes of yellow tide-foam. He found it in that book of poetry you brought into the kitchen. It begins "Up the airy mountain, Down the rushy glen, We daren't go a-hunting For fear of little men." It's the little men I keep thinking about.'

Penny was surprised. She had learned the poem about the Yonghy-Bonghy-Bò but she did not know that the others had looked at the book.

'Well, don't think about them, they're only in poetry. Think about ordinary things.'

Naomi was silent for quite a long time after that, then she whispered:

'I've been thinking about Stephan, though I wouldn't call him ordinary. Did you notice he stopped being foreign when he was frightened, he talked like us?'

Penny, now she thought about it, realized this was true.

'I always did think there was something phoney about him. When the boys are back we must have a rethink.'

'Turn him out do you mean?'

Penny had enough to worry about without Stephan.

'I don't know.' Then she clutched at Naomi's arm. 'Look!'
Though the girls did not know it they were at the turning
where the whole view up the water almost to the Atlantic
lay below them. What had caught her attention was a light
on either a boat or an island. 'I bet that's them. Come on,
hurry. Perhaps it's a beacon asking for help.'

24

The Island

THE tide had carried the boat, just as Aunt Dymphna had hoped, where they wished to go. First it had grated against a rock.

'Splendid!' Aunt Dymphna had called. She leant over the side and passed the lobster pot to Robin. 'Lower it, dear boy, I can feel a lobster waiting for his breakfast.' Then, after the pot was lowered, the boat had drifted on until gently it had touched a small island.

Aunt Dymphna appeared to have landed at islands in the dead of night all her life.

'Make the boat secure,' she ordered Alex. Then she gave a hand to the shivering Robin. 'Undress quickly, dear boy, and wrap yourself in my cloak. It is splendidly warm, it comes from a place called Bandon where once such capes were made. Alex, find something that will burn. We must have a fire, your brother is cold.'

Alex, struggling to secure the boat, could have shaken Aunt Dymphna. 'We must have a fire! Alex, find something that will burn.' Even in daylight it would be difficult to find anything that would burn, but in the dark it was nonsense to try, silly old coot! Out loud he said:

'Find what? It's pitch black.'

'Not quite, dear boy, there is the moon when she comes out from behind the clouds. There'll be some dried seaweed and perhaps some turf, even some wood. Use your nose, boy, use your nose. Remember your Chesterton:

> They haven't got no noses,
> The fallen sons of Eve;
> Even the smell of roses
> Is not what they supposes;

But more than mind discloses
And more than men believe.'

Though scratched and bruised in the search, to Alex's amazement, he did collect an armload of more or less burnable material, including the lucky find of a broken packing-case which must have drifted on to the island. 'But I'll give the old girl a surprise,' he thought. 'I bet she'll expect me to set this lot alight by rubbing two sticks together, she won't guess that since I've been in Reenmore I've taken to carrying matches.'

But Alex had no chance to triumph for when he staggered back feeling rather proud of his finds a fire was already going and round it Aunt Dymphna and Robin – wrapped in her cloak – were prancing while they chanted:

'How many miles to Babylon?
Three score miles and ten.
Can I get there by candlelight?
Yes, and back again.
If your heels are nimble and light,
You may get there by candlelight.'

Aunt Dymphna broke off chanting to call out to Alex:
'That will be enough fuel for the moment. Join us, dear boy. We shall dance until Robin is warm.'

Alex pretended he had not heard and instead fed the bonfire with the bits of broken packing-case. 'Lucky,' he thought, 'there's no one to see them or they would think they were mad; if Robin could see himself in that cloak!'

It was Robin who gave in first. He flung himself down by the fire.

'I'm boiling, Aunt Dymphna, truly I am.'

Aunt Dymphna sat down beside him. She stared up at the sky.

"A beautiful night. We should do this more often. An island is an ideal spot on which to spend a summer night.'

'You would think,' thought Alex, 'we had chosen to come here the way she's carrying on,' but he said nothing for it really was rather pleasant. Warmed by the bonfire, listening to the quiet lap-lap of the waves against the rocks, and now and again a little call from a sea-bird. Then behind them they heard a 'hoo'. Aunt Dymphna looked over her shoulder.

'We've disturbed one of the local inhabitants. That is a seal.'

Robin half got up.

'I wonder if we could see him. We had a seal near us on the beach who stayed simply hours. We sang "All things bright and beautiful" to him.'

Alex thought that needed explaining.

'Rather a soppy choice, Naomi chose it.'

'A very fine choice in my opinion,' said Aunt Dymphna. 'As we've woken him up he might like a little quiet singing.'

'What shall we sing?' Robin asked.

'The question is what do you know? Could you manage "Sweet and low" do you think? I fancy our seal might care for Tennyson.'

The boys had both sung the song at school and, led by Aunt Dymphna, they were able to keep up with her, Alex rather unwillingly for he felt a bit of a fool singing to an invisible seal.

'Gently now,' she said. 'Remember we are putting a seal to sleep, not waking him up.'

> 'Sweet and low, sweet and low,
>   Wind of the western sea,
> Low, low, breathe and blow,
>   Wind of the western sea!
> Over the rolling waters go,
> Come from the dying moon, and blow,
>   Blow him again to me;
> While my little one, while my pretty one, sleeps.'

'I thought that sounded nice,' Robin said when they had finished singing. 'I should think the seal liked it.'

'So should I,' Aunt Dymphna agreed. 'So should I.'

Her voice seemed part of the night and the lap-lap of the waves. They fell silent and presently Robin went to sleep.

Aunt Dymphna gently pulled the cloak down so that it covered his feet. Alex suddenly remembered the postcard he had found in the outhouse.

'Robin and I found a postcard written by our grandfather when Dad was a boy.'

Aunt Dymphna was again staring up at the sky.

'"Lily and I feel a bit anxious about you,"' she quoted. '"Do watch the situation, there is always a bed with us. John is such a big boy now." As you see, Alex, that card is written on my memory so I do not need to look at it. It was the last communication I had from my brother Alfred.'

Alex, not sure what to say, remarked politely:

'I never met my grandfather.'

Aunt Dymphna did not seem to have heard him for she followed her own thoughts.

'Robin is like my brother Alfred, a great talker he was. Couldn't keep a thing to himself.'

Alex looked down at what he could see of Robin. He was just going to agree that perhaps the grandfather he had never known was like him when he remembered Stephan. Robin had been startlingly silent about him. He had to be fair.

'Robin can keep a secret sometimes. You'd be surprised.'

Aunt Dymphna did not seem to have heard him for she said:

'I am afraid Penny will be anxious about you. Always worrying that girl, so foolish and so wasteful of time.'

Alex felt that was rather mean. Penny certainly was a fusser, but one way and another she had been given a good deal to fuss about since they came to Reenmore.

'She doesn't do badly, considering,' he said.

Aunt Dymphna sniffed.

'How delicious seaweed smells. She does very well considering she has no help from her brothers or her sister.'

Alex was indignant.

'We all help. One of us dries up after every meal and we would cook but she won't let us.'

'I understand that unhealthy synthetic material you all

wear nowadays almost washes itself. Why then is Penny trying to wash for the whole family?'

Alex knew he was flushing and was glad it was too dark for Aunt Dymphna to see.

'Boys don't do washing, besides I've been busy trying to catch things. I can't do everything.'

'Sailors take pride in doing their own laundry. Mind you, my dear boy, Penny is a fool, the more you do the more you may.

> Far and few, far and few,
> Are the lands where the Jumblies live;
> Their heads are green, and their hands are blue,
> And they went to sea in a Sieve.'

Alex boiled inside with rage. That was so like Aunt Dymphna, she never finished a conversation. First hinting they were not doing enough to help Penny, then talking about sailors, as if they had anything to do with it, and now quoting one of her poems which had no connexion with what they were talking about. Well, he would shame the old thing, he would show her they thought about her even if they didn't think so much about each other.

'We've got an address from Oonagh of a nursery and we are ordering plants for your herb garden.'

Aunt Dymphna got up.

'No, thank you, dear boy. Herbs should be gathered when the moon is full. Tonight, as you will observe when she comes out from behind the clouds, she is in her last quarter.' She flogged her arms across her chest and skipped a few steps. 'In spite of our bonfire it is a little chilly.'

For the first time Alex was conscious that Aunt Dymphna having wrapped Robin in her cape, was wearing only a thin black dress. He started to take off his pullover.

'Here, put this on. I'm quite warm.'

Aunt Dymphna gave him a light tap on the head.

'No, dear boy, no. I shall dance and that will keep me warm. If I wore your jersey you wouldn't dance, would you?'

Without waiting for an answer Aunt Dymphna skipped off out of sight.

Alex stayed on by the bonfire hugging his knees and feeling resentful. Why did Aunt Dymphna always make him feel in the wrong? At home everybody seemed to think he was doing all right. If only he could get her to talk about sensible things like school and marks and all that. Being able to spout poetry by the yard wasn't so important. Funny though about that postcard, she certainly had remembered what it said. Suddenly he began, for the first time, to wonder about Aunt Dymphna. Of course she was a queer old thing, mad as a hornet, but in a sort of way she was brave. It couldn't be much fun living all alone in Reenmore, especially as she seemed pretty poor and had no relations now except their father. He hoped the twenty-five pounds would last until they went home, he didn't want to have to embarrass the old thing by talking about money, and he'd have to if he had to ask her about cashing a cheque. Perhaps there was something more he could catch which would save buying food. He must find out about lobsters. What was it Aunt Dymphna had said?

Tis the voice of the Lobster; I heard him declare,
You have baked ...

When Aunt Dymphna came skipping back with more fuel she found Alex asleep with his head on his knees. Quietly she made up the fire, then she raised her arms to the moon, which had come out from behind a bank of cloud, and quoted Hilaire Belloc:

'the moon on my left and the dawn on my right.
My brother, good morning: my sister good night.'

Then, resting her head against a rock, she closed her eyes and in a matter of seconds she too was asleep.

25

Breakfast with Oonagh

OONAGH, when she came down in answer to the girls'
knocking, was more concerned about the lobster catchers
than Mrs O'Brien had been. But she thought the news of the
fire was good.

'Your aunt is shocking in a boat. She will treat them as if
she was on dry land. Let's go and look at this fire, if it's in
the right position they are on an island.'

One glance at the bonfire and she was satisfied.

'That's all right,' she told Penny comfortingly, 'come
back to my cottage and I'll make us something warm to
drink, then directly it's light we'll go out and bring them
home; if they've landed on an island I expect they'll need
a tow.'

Nothing is more magical than the sea in the very early
morning on what is going to be a fine day. The clouds that
had hidden the moon had disappeared in the night and the
sea looked like silver-green silk flecked with pink. But in spite
of everything looking so gorgeous Penny was still too fussed
to enjoy it.

'I can't think why they'd land unless they had an accident,'
she said.

Oonagh laughed.

'I expect it was some kind of accident. I wouldn't put it
past your aunt to fall in and, if that happened, I don't suppose the boys could get her back into the boat. She had no
right to take them out at night, very naughty of her.'

'If they're only all right,' said Penny, 'but somebody may
be hurt.' She didn't add that she felt it in her bones that
they were but that was what her bones were saying.

'Stop fussing,' Oonagh advised. 'I bet they're all right.
It's you and Naomi who will need to go back to bed.'

'If I know Robin,' said Naomi, 'he'll be starving. He's always hungry.'

Oonagh sounded pleased.

'Good. I've got a splendid collection of odds and ends I shall fry up for breakfast – bacon, sausages, mushrooms and eggs.'

'That's what we call a m-over,' said Naomi. 'It sounds gorgeous but Aunt Dymphna won't eat it, she eats things like toadstools and dead leaves.'

'She must manage with mushrooms and bread and butter, but help me to persuade her to stay for breakfast, she ought to have something hot after a night on an island.'

The island party were awake before the boat arrived and, under Aunt Dymphna's supervision, the boys had manoeuvred the boat out to the lobster pot and were hauling it in.

Hauling in a lobster pot is hard work, but though breathless, Robin managed to wonder about the lobster.

'If there is one how do we get it out of the pot?' he gasped.

'Pull it, dear boy, pull it. Do be careful or you'll upset the boat. Now heave.'

Presently the top of the pot appeared and then the whole of it. Robin gave an excited squeak.

'There's an enormous something inside but it isn't a lobster, it's nearly black.'

Aunt Dymphna, precariously balanced on a rock, peered into the pot.

'A splendid lobster! They are not red, dear boy, until they are cooked.'

Alex tried to sound calm.

'How did you say we got it out of the pot?'

'Hold it firmly by the back of the neck and persuade it out tail first.'

'Let's get the pot into the boat,' Alex whispered to Robin. 'It doesn't look to me as if it had a back of the neck to hold it by.'

When the pot was in the boat Aunt Dymphna, hopping with excitement, directed operations from her slippery rock.

'Robin, hold him by the tail. Alex, dear boy, as soon as the neck shows grip it firmly. The claws don't move backwards so they can't nip you if you hold him properly.'

Robin put a hand in the pot and gripped the lobster by the tail and persuaded it through the neck of the pot.

'I bet she falls in,' he whispered to Alex. 'I wish she'd stand still.'

'It might be easier if she did fall in,' Alex whispered back. 'Then she can be the one to get the lobster by the back of the neck.'

But Aunt Dymphna somehow kept her balance.

'Now!' she yelled to Alex. 'Grip him hard. Don't care how much he thrashes about he can't nip you.'

In the excitement neither Aunt Dymphna, Alex nor Robin heard the chug-chug of Oonagh's motor boat. Then suddenly Oonagh's voice rang out.

'Put the creature back in the pot, we'll put him in a wet sack at the cottage.'

Alex could have kissed her.

'Leave go of the tail,' he whispered to Robin. 'Thank goodness somebody with sense has turned up.'

But Robin, wild with excitement, was no longer hearing advice. Having got half the lobster out of the pot he was determined to finish the job. He gripped it by what Aunt Dymphna called the back of the neck and heaved it into the boat.

'Bravo, dear boy! Bravo!' boomed Aunt Dymphna and slid off the rock into the sea.

Oonagh took off her coat and, in spite of protests, succeeded in buttoning Aunt Dymphna into it and hauling her into her boat.

'You better join Alex,' she said to Penny, 'in the other boat. We'll have to tow her in as I see one of the oars is missing. Get ashore first and collect Robin's clothes and tell him to get into my boat.'

'What about the lobster?' Penny asked.

'We ought to tie its claws together,' Oonagh felt in her pockets and brought out a little coil of string. 'Tell Alex to make loops and slip them over the lobster's claws and draw them tight. That will keep him quiet, poor beast, until we get him into a sack.'

Penny carried out all her instructions but Alex struck at tying the lobster's claws together.

'We could push him away if he tries to bite us,' he whispered to Penny. 'They all expect you to do so many things at once in these parts. I've got to see the tow rope works.'

At the cottage Oonagh took complete charge. She sent first Aunt Dymphna and then Robin to have hot baths. She gave Alex a sack, told him to soak it in the sea and put the lobster in it. She told Penny to ring up the boat owner to tell him where the boat was.

'Don't mention an oar is missing. I'll go out later to look for it. You come and help me cook the m-over, Naomi. I'm sure you and Penny need a good breakfast even if the lobster catchers don't.'

Robin's clothes had been nearly dry lying next to the bonfire, and Oonagh gave them a final drying on a horse in front of a very cheering turf fire. So when Aunt Dymphna appeared after her bath she had her cloak back. She flapped it, as was her habit.

'I appreciate the bath, Oonagh, but I must be off. From what Penny says that poor tinker woman needs me. I have treated her before – a splendid mixture: burnet, costmary, just a touch of fennel and some rue. Puts her right in no time.'

Oonagh tried to stop her.

'Can't you wait until the children have finished their breakfast? Penny and Naomi have done enough running about for today.'

'I don't want them to run about. I have a plan. If you can find Eamon-the-fish get another lobster and the children can feast like Lucullus on lobster on the beach. Some time I could drive back and pick them up.'

Oonagh had left the table and gone to the door with Aunt Dymphna.

'I think the lobster lunch is a splendid idea. But I'll run the children home, I know you when you get amongst the tinkers, you've no idea of time.'

Aunt Dymphna gave her cloak another flap.

'I should hope not. I have no use for time.' Then she was gone.

At the table the children had exchanged anxious looks and kicks, which asked: what on earth were they to do about Stephan?

Oonagh came back laughing.

'I adore your aunt. I hate to think what fearful concoction she is going to give the poor tinker's wife but it will probably cure her.'

'After breakfast,' said Alex, 'I think Robin and I will have to go to Reenmore – it's to fetch our bathing things.'

The other three made approving noises.

'It is too good a day to miss bathing,' Penny added.

Oonagh poured herself out another cup of tea.

'All right, I gather you boys slept on the island so you

won't mind the walk. Would you girls like a lie-down here or on the beach?'

'The beach,' said Naomi. 'If we were on beds we might sleep all the morning and miss bathing.'

'Right,' Oonagh agreed. 'And my plan is you come back here for lunch. I've a smashing lobster dish I make, it will be more interesting than eating it cold.'

After breakfast Penny managed to catch Alex alone for a moment while they were helping to clear the table.

'Hard boil four eggs and give him some bread and butter and a jug of milk. Tell him he'll have a proper supper tonight.'

Alex nodded.

'O.K. He'll start to cluck soon with all the eggs he's got inside him.'

While she was washing up and the children were drying and putting away Oonagh turned on the wireless to get the English news. It was extraordinary to hear a wireless again. It was a sort of background noise at home but now they were so used to not having it that they had not noticed that they had no idea what was happening in the outside world.

'Anything could have happened and we wouldn't know,' Robin told Oonagh. 'You know, like someone having tried to blow up the Houses of Parliament like Guy Fawkes did.'

Oonagh laughed.

'You'd have heard about that all right. It's the silly season, you know who has been chosen as Beauty Queen and poor fools who boat and bathe without being able to swim and get themselves drowned. Hush now, and let me hear.'

The news was as boring as Oonagh had said it would be. The children crept about the kitchen on tiptoe putting away the frying pan, the silver and the plates. Then suddenly they stood still as statues. 'There is still no news of Oswald Wallington, the schoolboy film star who has been missing for four weeks. People will have seen the boy on films and so will recognize him. He is fair, looks less than his age, which is twelve; he has unusually large blue eyes. The boy was to have given up his career to attend a famous boarding school but after one visit to the school he disappeared. The police have not dismissed the possibility of kidnapping, or murder, but are still inclined to the theory that the boy is in hiding. Anybody who may have seen the boy or may have any information about him is asked to communicate with New Scotland Yard, Whitehall 1212, or any police station.'

Poor Robin, he had been marvellous at keeping Stephan a secret, but hearing the wireless announcement made him over-excited.

'It's him!' he burst out. 'I told you I'd seen him before. I told you so.'

Alex was angry. Why couldn't Robin have held his tongue a little longer?

'When did you tell us? I don't remember.'

That, Robin thought, was the last straw.

'Of course you remember. It was at breakfast and you didn't believe me and Naomi when we said we'd seen him before so I said all right, don't believe me but you'll be sorry, for there was something else I noticed which I was going to tell you and I didn't.'

'What?' Alex asked.

'That he wasn't foreign, it was made-up foreign for sometimes he forgot.'

Alex remembered then and wished, more than Robin would ever know, that he had believed the family sleuth and listened to what he had to say.

26

The Hunt is Up

OONAGH was angry. The children had found Stephan a nuisance, and they had not liked him, but that anyone would say they were silly and irresponsible amazed them. But Oonagh, with her blue eyes blazing as if there were fireworks in them, disillusioned them.

'How could you be such unutterable idiots? Surely, before you hid an unknown boy, you might have asked your aunt if you might.'

Penny tried to make Oonagh see how it had happened.

'It was the day after we arrived and we didn't know Aunt Dymphna, and you do see she's not easy to talk to, even now.'

'No, I don't,' Oonagh stormed. 'You're an ungrateful lot of brats. Here is a great-aunt you don't know turning her house upside down for you and in return you get her into trouble with the police.'

Robin, painfully conscious it was he who had spilled the beans, said crossly:

'I don't think anyone who was fair could say our Aunt Dymphna had turned her house upside down for us. We wouldn't like to be rude but the bit of the house where we live, is absolutely terrible, though no worse than her part, it's all awful.'

'There are more important things than furniture,' Oonagh stormed. 'There is privacy. Your aunt loves her privacy yet when she was asked to have you four she never hesitated. When she came to me to borrow bed linen she said: "This is my duty, Oonagh, and however distasteful I shall do it."'

The children were so surprised they were silenced. Ever since they had been in Reenmore they had felt that they were brave and uncomplaining, never once in their letters to their father and mother had they hinted how awful Reenmore was, and how hard they were expected to work. Now it took their breath away to hear that a sensible person like Oonagh was on Aunt Dymphna's side, and thought it was she who was suffering by having them in her house.

At last Penny said:

'Children have to go somewhere when something like what happened to us happens.'

'Of course,' Oonagh agreed, 'and your aunt accepted it, but the children needn't be quite such a hopeless, incompetent lot as you are.'

Robin was not taking that. Penny might not be a good cook but she had tried, and in spite of no help from Aunt Dymphna they had been fed.

'In England children who are at school haven't time to cook and clean and wash, which at Reenmore Penny's had to do. And whatever you think, we think Penny's done pretty well.'

Unkindness can be taken with grace, it is kindness that breaks down the reserves. To her shame, after Robin's outburst, Penny found tears running down her cheeks.

Naomi who, almost dry-eyed had faced the terrors of the kitchen garden at night, could not take Penny's tears. She dashed at Oonagh and, shaken with sobs, beat her with her fists.

'You are mean, horribly mean. It's loathsome at Reenmore – it's dirty and there's no furniture, everything that's been bearable is because of what Penny's done. I don't care what you think about Stephan, he's a horrible boy, we never wanted to look after him, it was only goodness that made us.'

Alex, humbled beyond bearing by what Oonagh had said about them, felt he must try and explain about Stephan.

'You see, if he had escaped from a Communist country it did seem we had to hide him however revolting he was. I can't explain about Aunt Dymphna but truly she didn't seem the sort of person you could tell things to.'

Suddenly Oonagh stopped being angry and was just exhausted.

'Of course I forgot that in Reenmore you don't hear the wireless and you never see the papers. The story blew up when you arrived. The boy's film contract was finished and it was decided to send him to an English public school where he has a cousin. He spent a Saturday afternoon with the cousin, who evidently took a scunner to him and fed him ridiculous stories of what happened in the school and, as a result, he ran away. The question is what do we do now? How can we hand him over to the police with the least possible disturbance to your aunt?'

Penny, still sniffing and moping, said:

'Could you come with us and see him? We'll do anything you say but as you'll see, Stephan isn't easy.'

'I've gathered that from the papers,' Oonagh agreed. "He is, I read, a spoilt little horror, that is why his sensible parents decided he needed a boarding school. If more sensible parents would decide the same way there might be less juvenile criminals.'

When the family and Oonagh arrived at Reenmore they found Stephan had worked himself up to a frenzied condition of self-pity.

'Beasts!' he had kept muttering. 'If only they knew who I was they'd crawl on their knees to bring me things. First they leave me alone in this dreadful house all night, and then they don't come back to give me my breakfast. I hope those nasty boys are drowned, it will serve them right.' So it made Stephan take a mental somersault when he realized that the four children and the strange lady who marched into the room had not come to apologize for the discomfort he was enduring – quite the opposite.

'I knew I'd seen you before,' Robin said, 'and I knew you didn't really talk foreign. Naomi and me saw you in a film.'

'And we didn't like you in it,' Naomi added.

Oonagh sat on the edge of the bed.

'We know all about you. Have you the faintest idea of the trouble you've caused?'

Stephan looked sulky.

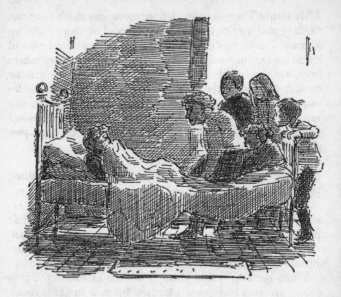

'I couldn't go to that horrible school. They beat you. Nobody there knew who I was and they didn't care.'

'You have hidden yourself in somebody's house without their knowledge,' Oonagh went on, 'which is a criminal offence. If I did the right thing I should hand you over to the police and have you charged with illegal entry, and no doubt you would be sent to Borstal.'

Stephan was in bed. He shrank under the bedclothes staring at Oonagh with terrified eyes.

'They hid me. It's their fault as much as mine.'

Oonagh's voice could roar like a lion.

'Be quiet, you horrible child. These children only took you in because you lied to them. If anybody ever knows of the lies you have told I dread to think what might happen to you. But they are generous children and don't want to hurt you in spite of all the trouble you have caused. In fact, if you do what I tell you, I don't believe they will report your conduct to the police.'

Only Stephan's scared eyes showed above the sheets.

'What am I to do?'

Oonagh sounded like a judge.

'Miss Gareth is out so now is your chance. Get dressed and run up the lane. At the top you will find a house, in it lives a Mrs O'Brien – tell her the truth, who you are, and she will hand you over to the police and they will see you get back to your parents. But if you dare say one word about where you have been hiding I shall go to the police and charge you with false pretences and then you will be locked up. The choice is up to you.'

In spite of the fact that none of the children liked Stephan and he had been a fearful nuisance they were sorry for him at that moment. After all, he was a film star with an international reputation and it must be humiliating to be kicked out of the house. Curiously Stephan, who was after all a good actor, did not take the opportunity to make a handsome exit. Instead he fell back on his usual sulks plus a most unmanly whimpering.

'I think you're awfully mean. I'm only a little boy. How would you like to be sent to a school where they beat you?'

Oonagh looked at him with disgust.

'Get up and get dressed, you nasty child.' Then she turned to Penny. 'It would be kind of you and Naomi if you would get him a cup of tea and something to eat. He doesn't deserve it but we may as well be charitable. Goodness knows when he'll get his next meal.'

Oonagh sent Robin-the-sleuth into the lane to watch for Aunt Dymphna's return. From the window the family watched Stephan slink across the field and disappear out of sight.

'It seems mean,' said Penny, 'to push him on to poor Mrs O'Brien.'

Oonagh laughed.

'Don't worry about that. She'll be thrilled – a real film star under the roof. Nothing so exciting has ever happened to her before. You watch, in a few minutes' time Mary and

Sheila will be haring down the road to fetch the police as if the hounds of hell were behind them. I wish I thought Stephan would be treated as he deserves but he won't be, any minute now Mrs O'Brien will start to kill the fatted calf.'

27

The Cable

O N E way and another life was much easier after Stephan, as they still called him, had gone. It was not just that there was no Stephan to hide or feed, it was that the children managed better themselves. It is sickening when you have thought you were bearing up well under intolerable conditions to hear yourselves described as 'a hopeless, incompetent lot'. Not that on talking it over the children thought Oonagh had been fair, in fact they agreed she had been pretty mean, surprisingly so for somebody so nice, but things have been said both by Oonagh and Aunt Dymphna which had sunk in.

The morning after Stephan had gone Penny planned a big wash. This was partly because it was a miserable day not fit for bathing, but also to prove to herself that she was not incompetent, whatever the others might be. Then Alex turned up. He spoke in a voice which tried to sound as if he was saying the sort of thing he said every day.

'Give me my things, I'll wash them myself.'

Penny was annoyed for it is annoying when you are trying to show how competent you are – or at least can be – when somebody else chips in being competent too.

'Boys don't do washing.'

'That's all you know, sailors always do their own. And while I'm doing mine I might as well do Robin's at the same time. He's a bit young to do his.'

Penny, not knowing what Aunt Dymphna had said on the island, was amazed past argument.

'Oh, all right. I get water to wash them in from the O'Briens' well, ours is too brown.'

Alex's attempt to help Penny did not stop at doing his own and Robin's washing, he made a bigger effort and made

Robin do the same about keeping their room tidy. Robin was furious.

'You're getting as bad as Penny. Fuss, fuss, fuss.'

Robin had never accepted Oonagh's statement that they were a hopeless, incompetent lot. He still thought Penny had managed well considering and it was nonsense to say the rest of them were incompetent, children weren't expected to be competent. But inside he was angry with himself. He had been so sure he was a good sleuth, it was pretty sickening to find that most of the boys he had played with had known that Oswald Wallington, the film star, was missing, and had never said a word about it. It was more sickening, that when he had kept the secret for such ages that Stephan was in the house, he should have let it out in front of Oonagh.

It was more than maddening that it was so difficult, without showing he had a special interest in Stephan, to find out what had happened to him after he left Reenmore. The beginning was easy for Mrs O'Brien had come rushing in bursting with her news.

'And who do you think was in my kitchen this very day? Oswald Wallington! I knew who he was the very moment he put his face round my door. Oh, he is a beautiful boy though too pale. I sent Mary and Sheila running for the Garda and then I asked would he fancy something to eat. The poor child, it is starved he has been.'

The children could not face hearing the fairy stories Stephan had told Mrs O'Brien so, knowing a Garda was an Irish policeman, they asked about him.

'What did the Garda do with Steph ... I mean with Oswald Wallington?' Alex wanted to know.

'I am not knowing,' Mrs O'Brien had said regretfully. 'But I think he was taken in a motor car to Bantry.'

Nobody seemed to know or care what happened to Stephan once he left for Bantry but stories flew to and fro and Robin recounted them all.

'Do you know, he said he lived with tinkers. Imagine, he said he had nothing to eat but blackberries! And when I think of all those eggs! He said he hid in a church. He told the Garda that part of the time he was in a broken-down old house. I bet he meant Reenmore. Lucky Aunt Dymphna didn't hear him.'

Then one day Robin came home with a newspaper Oonagh had given him. Stephan was no longer front-page news but he was mentioned in a paragraph inside. It was headed 'Missing film-star schoolboy.' Then it said: 'Oswald Wallington, the boy film star, who was in hiding in Ireland, has been sent to a crammer to prepare him for his first term at a public school.'

'I hope that crammer is so strict he couldn't be stricter,' said Robin. 'I thought he was a horrible boy.'

Penny, in the next few weeks, struggled to be a better cook. It was not so easy for it was seldom she had anything to cook which wanted grand cooking. Most weeks there was a joint of beef or lamb, and Penny had learnt what to do with them. You ate the joint roasted the first day with potatoes cooked in the gravy. The next day you ate it cold with potatoes in their jackets. The third day you minced what was left and put potatoes on top and made a cottage pie. She did think of making something more original than the cottage pie, but the cookery book suggested using ingredients which made Bernadette-the-shop think she was crazy.

'Is it walnut liquor and mushroom ketchup you are wanting? I never heard tell of them things hereabouts, and I doubt if you would buy the like in the city of Dublin.'

However, Penny did experiment with mackerel which Alex caught in increasing numbers as August passed and it was September. Unfortunately the cookery book never allowed for anybody catching their own fish, it took it for granted all fish came from shops. 'Use,' it said in an authoritative tone as if it was easy to do, 'mackerel of medium size.' What was medium size, Penny wondered? Alex's mackerel varied from quite small to fairly large. Another recipe said: 'Ingredients. One large mackerel.' Well, how large was large? However, undeterred by not knowing,

Penny struggled on. 'Do not wash the fish,' one recipe ordered, 'but wipe it clean and dry.' Mackerel were clean already and why wouldn't they be coming straight from the sea? But dry, with what did you dry a mackerel when you only had two drying cloths – one you had washed and one in use? But it was the sauces which really foxed Penny. What was Béchamel sauce? How did you make any sauce without lumps in it? And what in the world was a sauté pan?

The family bore Penny's efforts almost without complaint but when she tried pickling the mackerel they could take no more.

'Everybody,' said Alex, laying down his fork, 'knows you are trying but truthfully the mackerel were all right when you didn't try but just cooked them.'

Penny knew her pickled mackerel were raw and so disgusting, but she did not want to be told so.

'I hadn't got twelve peppercorns, which the book said I ought to have, and I didn't have bay leaves so I used some of Aunt Dymphna's leaves, but I dare say they aren't the same, and there isn't an earthenware baking dish.'

Robin was hungry so he struggled to eat his mackerel.

'It is absolutely revolting. If you ask me I think you forgot whatever it ought to have been soaked in.'

'I didn't ask you,' said Penny. 'As a matter of fact, if you don't like the fish blame Alex, the book says mackerel are best when the fish are not full grown. I think these were not just full grown, they were old.'

'Whatever they were I vote we put them in the pig bucket,' Naomi suggested, 'and have eggs.'

But Penny's worst failures were puddings, especially the sort that were meant to stand up. It was an apple snow which finally made the family put their feet down. It should have turned out right because Penny had all the ingredients and she did what the book said – or she thought she did. But however much she whipped the snow refused to stand up as promised, and even when poured into glasses it looked odd.

'What is this?' Alex asked. 'Soup?'

'Mine is lemon peel in sweet egg,' said Naomi.

Even Robin couldn't eat that snow.

'Mine just tastes of raw egg. Truly, Penny, don't try any more. We like fruit out of tins.'

Penny struggled to pretend she didn't care but inside she did.

'I am a failure,' she thought. 'No wonder Oonagh said we were incompetent for I certainly am.'

It had happened so gradually that the other three had not noticed how Naomi had changed since she came to Reenmore. It was so long since she had made a scene about anything they had forgotten the Naomi who made a scene at the drop of a hat. But Naomi knew she had changed and she knew when it had happened, it was the night the tinker came and she had been brave enough to walk alone in the dark to fetch Mrs O'Brien. Nobody could be as brave as she had been that night and go back to being a cry-baby, at least not unless you cried on purpose because it was the way to get what you wanted.

Aunt Dymphna had been more elusive than usual since the night on the island. The tinker's wife had not got well quickly and had needed more than one visit and several different kinds of medicine. Then the herbs began to give out and Aunt Dymphna was away at full moon time collecting some more.

'And I shall get plants too for our splendid garden,' she told the children during one of her flying visits to the kitchen. 'I would take you too but I got such a scolding from Oonagh when I took you boys out to catch a lobster. Pity. Lovely work herb-gathering by moonlight.'

There were two hard-working days following the herb-gathering when the children helped plant out the herb garden.

'Wonderful tales had our fathers of old—
    Wonderful tales of the herbs and the stars—
The Sun was Lord of the Marigold,
    Basil and Rocket belonged to Mars.

> Pat as a sum in division it goes—
> (Every plant had a star bespoke)—
> Who but Venus should govern the Rose?
> Who but Jupiter own the Oak?

Dear, dear Kipling. So understanding,' said Aunt Dymphna. The children, inwardly groaning, were too exhausted to answer for Aunt Dymphna accepted no excuses when it came to her herb garden, and anyway believed planting it to be fun.

'Splendid, dears! Splendid!' she said when the children paused to mop their foreheads. 'Where I could I took fifty or so plants, that is to be sure at least one will take.'

'She may have thought she just took fifty plants,' Penny said afterwards, 'but I think she took a hundred.'

Sometimes on a flying visit to the children Aunt Dymphna actually praised. One day she gave Penny's head an awkward little pat.

'I've been looking at my fuchsia hedge.

> And you shall wash your linen and keep your body white
> In rainfall at morning and dewfall at night.'

'That's my piece of poetry,' said Naomi.

Penny felt embarrassed.

'Alex washed his and Robin's and it isn't rainfall, it's Mrs O'Brien's well.'

Another day Aunt Dymphna blew in to congratulate Alex.

'As Shakespeare had it "I smell a very ancient and fish-like smell." My seagulls are complaining, Alex. They say you are clearing the bay of prawns and that no less than five lobsters have come into my house.'

'You were away,' Alex apologized. 'There was one for you.'

'But as you weren't here,' Robin said, 'we ate it. I'm always starving in this place.'

'I didn't get them by myself,' Alex explained. 'I went out several mornings early helping Eamon-the-fish. He said five were my share.'

The weather was glorious that September. The children lived out of doors, each busy with their own things. What Aunt Dymphna had told Penny proved to be true – time did not matter in Ireland. So if they ate a picnic lunch at half past eleven, had tea at three and supper at half past six and a late snack at nine nobody minded.

'The only thing that has time here is church,' said Naomi. 'I can't think how Aunt Dymphna knows it's church time for all she has is a dandelion clock.'

But Aunt Dymphna did know time on Sundays and very embarrassing the children found it. For it was her opinion that the vicar should only preach for a quarter of an hour. When this was up she made it clear that she was not pleased. She got up and drew her cloak round her as if she was leaving. If that failed she got up again and this time gave her cloak a flap. If this too failed, which it seldom did for the vicar did not believe in long sermons either, she gestured to the children to show they should get ready to leave. Sunday after Sunday the children were scarlet to the ears with embarrassment but the vicar did not seem to mind. When he shook hands after the service with the congregation he nearly always said something to Aunt Dymphna, such as: 'Sorry I was a bit long,' or 'I thought you really were walking out this time.'

But, except on Sundays, one golden day slipped into another and time stood still. It was therefore a terrific shock when one day when the children came back from the beach they found Aunt Dymphna standing in the lane waving a cable.

'Your parents are coming home. Isn't it splendid?'

Of course the children knew from the letters they had every week that their father was better – but coming home, that was a real surprise!

'When?' Penny asked.

'Next Wednesday, and I am to book places for you on the aeroplane on the Friday.'

Robin felt a cable was a dull way for Aunt Dymphna to get the news.

'Hadn't your seagulls told you they were coming home?'

'Of course, dear boy, of course. This cable merely confirms what I already knew.'

Aunt Dymphna flapped off across the field. The children stared at each other. Home. Back to Medway. Back to school.

'Of course it will be gorgeous to see Daddy and Mummy,' said Robin speaking for them all. 'But now we're going I feel sort of sorry and glad mixed, which is something I never expected to feel about Reenmore.'

28

Presents

THE last day but three, lying on the beach after lunch Alex said:

'I think we ought to give Aunt Dymphna a good-bye present. Anybody got any ideas?'

Naomi could not imagine Aunt Dymphna opening a parcel.

'She's not really a present sort of person.'

'Unless we could get her a herb she hasn't got,' Robin suggested.

But it was Penny who found the answer.

'You know how keen she is on poetry.'

Alex groaned.

'Not another book, her floors are covered with them already.'

'I wasn't thinking of giving a book,' Penny explained, 'I was thinking of learning poetry for her. We could each say something in the car on the way to the airport. She'd like that.'

'I shan't have to learn anything new,' said Naomi. 'I shall say "I will make you brooches."'

'Better watch out how you say it then,' Alex reminded her, 'or she'll tell her gulls to peck out your eyes and tear out your liver.'

'What'll you say, Alex?' asked Penny.

Alex remembered the night Aunt Dymphna had cooked the toadstools.

' "Up the airy mountain." '

'It's rather mean to choose it,' said Penny, 'because I've already learnt it, but I think it's so Aunt Dymphna-ish I must say the Yonghy-Bonghy-Bò.'

'What will you say, Robin?' Naomi asked.

'I shan't say, I shall sing,' said Robin. 'It will be "Sweet and low" like we sang to that seal on the island.'

Now that they were going home Penny saw herself and the others more as her mother would see them and she realized something must be done. She must wash her own and Naomi's hair; sea water had done all right while they were at Reenmore where there was nobody to care how they looked, but Mummy would have a fit. As for the boys they looked like badly groomed long-haired pop singers. Alex had cut some of his front hair when it got in his eyes, but Robin had not even done that and the piece of hair on the crown of his head was so long it stood up like a young tree.

It was not easy to get the family to see that hairdressing was necessary. Even Naomi, who usually was so fussy about her appearance, rebelled.

'Oh, no! We've not got to start dressing up yet. Mummy will take us to a proper hairdresser when we get home.'

'Where on earth do you think we could get our hair cut?' Alex asked. 'What a fusser you are, Penny.'

'I'll fix mine down with water the day we go,' Robin promised. 'It looks less long like that.'

But Penny was determined not to let her family arrive home looking like savages – so determined that the next morning immediately after breakfast she found the courage to go to Aunt Dymphna's side of the house to ask her for help. 'Though of course she won't help,' she thought. 'I expect she'll just tell me what a fool I am to worry.'

Aunt Dymphna was in her dining-room sorting out the game called 'Who knows?'

'There you are, dear,' she said, just as if she had sent for Penny. 'This is such a splendid game and we have never played it. I think you must take it home with you.'

'How do you play it?' Penny asked.

Aunt Dymphna picked some large cards marked out in squares out of the 'Who knows?' box.

'Each player has one of these big cards. Then somebody asks the questions.' She held out a bag. 'The questions and answers are written on little tickets in this bag. They are drawn from the bag by whoever asks the questions and each time a right answer is given the player receives the ticket, which he places on one of the squares on his card. The first full card is the winner.'

'What sort of questions?' Penny asked. 'It sounds rather like lessons.'

'Splendid questions.' Aunt Dymphna took out a few from the bag. 'Listen to this. What is ink made of?'

'I don't know.'

'Then I'll read out the answer. "Gall, copper ash, gum arabic and water." That's a useful thing to know, isn't it?'

'I suppose so,' Penny agreed doubtfully, 'or at least it's an odd thing to know.'

'Or how about this?' Aunt Dymphna held out another ticket. 'What is the date of the creation of the world?"'

'I'm afraid I don't know that either.'

'"4004 B.C." Most interesting. Now try this one. "What is indigo?"'

'Isn't it a paint?'

Aunt Dymphna dropped the ticket in the bag.

'The right answer is "The leaves of an Asian plant." Are you any good on trains? How about this? "What is the standard gauge of British railway trains?"'

Penny shook her head.

'If I ever knew I've forgotten.'

'"Four feet eight and a half inches."' Aunt Dymphna dropped the ticket in the bag and put the bag and cards back in the box.

'Take it, dear child. A splendid occupation for you all on winter evenings.'

Penny took the box unwillingly for she could see it would be difficult to squeeze it into her suitcase, and nobody would play the game when she got it home.

'I came to see you because I was wondering if before we go, we could drive to some place where I could get the boys' hair cut.'

'Barber, barber, shave a pig,
How many hairs will make a wig?
Four and twenty, that's enough,
Give the barber a pinch of snuff.'

Penny felt unusually brave with Aunt Dymphna that
morning. It was difficult standing in her terrible dining-
room, with its cascading cobwebs and dust lying like moss,
to hold on to the fact that there was the home world where
things like how hair looked mattered. It was impossible to
be really firm because in a sort of way she was sorry for Aunt
Dymphna. With her wobbly little table and her one rickety
chair she truly was like the Yonghy-Bonghy-Bò, and however strange they had found her at first she had been kind in
her own way.

'I do see that it sounds silly here to fuss about hair and
things like that. Neither Alex nor Robin are fussing, it's
just me, they'd be happy to say "How many hairs will make
a wig?" But I know how they're going to look to Mummy.'

'Don't worry, child. I had hoped that worried frown was
gone for good, probably if you stayed here it would vanish
for ever, but now your face is turned for home it is coming
back. I have an idea. This afternoon we will go to Bantry.'

Bantry had become a fairy-tale place, the sort you could
talk about but could never reach. When they had first come
to Reenmore they were always saying 'When we go to Bantry.' But in the last weeks no one had mentioned it. It was a
splendid idea to go to Bantry but Penny could see she would
have a job with the family.

'Thanks awfully. I'd better go and tell the others or they
will all have gone out.'

It was – always allowing for the terror of driving with
Aunt Dymphna – a lovely ride into Bantry. It was impossible
to believe it was the same journey which had so terrified
them on the night they had arrived. It was an unlucky
day to have chosen to go to Bantry for there had been
a fair so they continually met cattle being driven to new
homes.

'Fools!' Aunt Dymphna roared at the men in charge as,

without slowing down, she zigzagged her Austin round bullocks. 'Leave those creatures to look after themselves. Never interfere, they have more sense than you have.'

Every house and cottage had a dog on the watch that afternoon who dashed out at the car. The children were of course ready for them and hung out of the windows yelling, 'We're going to Bantry,' and as usual the system worked.

Alex had not handed out regular pocket money while they had been at Reenmore, partly because he was not sure how far the money would go and partly because there was nothing much to spend it on. But now they were going home he felt safe to give each of them ten shillings.

'As we've got to waste an afternoon in Bantry we might as well buy some presents. I want to get some new fishing hooks for Eamon-the-fish.'

'And we must get something nice for Mrs O'Brien,' said Penny.

'And something for Daddy and Mummy,' Robin reminded them.

In Bantry Aunt Dymphna proved just as elusive as she was in the house. She parked her car outside the garage, flicked her cloak and vanished up the street calling out:

'See you here later.'

'Silly old thing!' said Alex. 'Why can't she say a time? What is later?' But he did not expect an answer for they were all used to Aunt Dymphna by now.

The hair-cutting over, the afternoon was spent shopping. After a great deal of arguing they bought Mrs O'Brien a teapot all over roses.

'She's certain to like it,' Naomi said, 'for she's always drinking tea.'

Oonagh proved more difficult but in the end they chose her a pen and pencil set.

'Nobody can have too many of those,' Robin pointed out, 'and most other things have "A present from Ireland" on them, which she wouldn't want.'

They bought their mother some handkerchiefs with a shamrock on them and their father a plain one with a J on

the corner. Then they separated to buy their personal presents.

'But do save a little to get something for Aunt Dymphna,' said Penny. 'Poetry saying was all right when we weren't giving presents, but now we can't leave her out.'

The others agreed and it was finally settled they should each contribute two shillings, but when it came to spending the money they had a terrible job to find anything suitable. They went all round the gift shops picking up plaster leprechauns, brooches with shamrock on them and money-boxes made like pigs covered in shamrocks.

'It's hopeless,' said Alex. 'There's nothing here she'd use.'

It was then Penny had an idea.

'We're in the wrong place. There must be somewhere sells second-hand things, like she'd buy in a sale.'

They found the sort of shop Penny meant. There was a

nice man in charge who did not mind how much they looked and turned over.

'Be searching to your heart's content,' he said. 'There is the day before you so where is the need to be hurrying yourselves.'

It was Robin who found the present and once seen there was no doubt of its perfection. It was what looked like an old-fashioned egg-timer. It stood on a black stand and the timer swung over a steel rod. But whatever it was originally made for it was not for cooking eggs for it was marked 'Fifteen Minutes.'

'Look! Look what I've found!' Robin shouted. 'A sermon timer. It's absolutely made for Aunt Dymphna.'

The man only wanted five shillings for that perfect present so the children spent the rest on ice-cream and cakes then, full and satisfied, they stood round the car until Aunt Dymphna, with a bird-like swoop, arrived from nowhere.

'Quick! Quick!' she said, as if it was they who had kept her waiting. '*Tempus Fugit.*' Then, looking first at Alex and then at Robin: 'Poor boys! So Penny has done her worst. What horrors you look! Let us sing all the way home to get the taste of barbers out of our nostrils. Get in. Get in.'

29

Good–bye to Reenmore

IT was all over. The good-byes, the present-giving, except Aunt Dymphna's present, and everybody seemed sorry to see them go.

'But I think this place is like sand,' said Penny. 'You are there when you're there, but when we've gone it's like the sea going out – all the marks which were us won't show any more.'

Robin did not like that.

'Not my marks won't. They'll remember me for ever.'

Naomi agreed with him.

'I think those girls I played with will remember me. They all said so when I gave them their good-bye sweets.'

Alex was uncertain.

'Eamon-the-fish was awfully pleased with the hooks and spinners and in a way he'll remember, but not to be sure what my name was.'

Drives with Aunt Dymphna never changed but that one was a little different because between shouting 'Road Hog' or 'We're going to the airport at Cork' they had to find time to say their poems. Naomi started with 'I will give you brooches.'

'That is better,' Aunt Dymphna said when she came to the last line. 'Never forget my seagulls. They can't stand affection.'

This annoyed Naomi.

'Saying that was part of our good-bye present. You should be polite about a present. We've each learnt a poem for you.'

'It's a sad day when one can only hear poetry as a present,' said Aunt Dymphna. 'Well, who is next?'

Penny said cautiously.

'I was going to say "On the Coast of Coromandel". But

truly it's only partly a present, most of it is because I like it.'

Aunt Dymphna shot across the road thereby scaring the heart out of the driver of a creamery lorry.

'Road Hog!' she shouted. Then to Penny: 'Go on, my dear girl. I shall enjoy this.'

There was no danger of Penny sounding affected, she just spoke the lines. But, though Aunt Dymphna did not know it, there was almost a lump in her throat when she reached the end:

> 'On that little heap of stone,
> To her Dorking Hens she moans,
> For the Yonghy-Bonghy-Bò,
> For the Yonghy-Bonghy-Bò.'

for old Aunt Dymphna was in many ways so like a Yonghy-Bonghy-Bò.

Robin sang next 'Sweet and Low'. It was not a very pleasant noise for he sang too fast and without expression. At the end Aunt Dymphna gave a honking laugh.

'Thank you, Robin. "Never anything can be amiss, When simpleness and duty tender it." Shakespeare said that but I am not sure I agree with him. Now, Alex, what have you got for me?'

'That poetry about the little men,' said Naomi. 'He will say it though he knows it frightens me.'

'Fripperies and fancies!' said Aunt Dymphna. 'You will have to be careful, Naomi, or you will grow up an ass. Come along, Alex. "Up the airy mountain, Down the rushy glen."'

Alex was embarrassed when he said poetry. And, though he had tried to learn it, there were so many nicer things to do at Reenmore he had not given enough time to it. But it did not matter. Aunt Dymphna knew every word and was delighted to recite it with him.

'Splendid, dear boy! Splendid!

> Wee folk, good folk,
> Trooping all together;
> Green jacket, red cap,
> And white owl's feather!

You have not been here long enough to know them but to me they are old friends. At some moment when I have time to look them out I shall post you each a book of poetry.'

The children thought of Reenmore – those vast piles of dusty, apparently unopened books. It was hard to believe Aunt Dymphna would ever have time to sort them, and harder still to believe that she would get to a post office to send them off.

They arrived early at the airport. The children had allowed for this. In the entrance hall they gave Aunt Dymphna her parcel. They stood round while she opened it. Would she like it? Would she want any sort of present? As Aunt Dymphna removed the string and brown paper the timer came into view.

'It's not for eggs, we knew you wouldn't want one of those,' Robin burst out. 'It's a sermon timer. It takes exactly fifteen minutes, we've timed it.'

Aunt Dymphna gave the sermon timer a little pat. She seemed as if she was trying to say something. Then she gave her cloak a flap, tossed back her head and she was gone.

The children stared after Aunt Dymphna but they said nothing. Then, as one person, they went to the desk to have their luggage weighed. Ireland was over – they belonged to London now.

JELLYBEAN *Tessa Duder*

A sensitive modern novel about Geraldine, alias 'Jellybean', who leads a rather solitary life as the only child of a single parent. She's tired of having to fit in with her mother's busy schedule, but a new friend and a performance of 'The Nutcracker Suite' change everything.

THE PRIESTS OF FERRIS *Maurice Gee*

Susan Ferris and her cousin Nick return to the world of O which they had saved from the evil Halfmen, only to find that O is now ruled by cruel and ruthless priests. Can they save the inhabitants of O from tyranny? An action-packed and gripping story by the author of prize-winning THE HALFMEN OF O.

THE SEA IS SINGING *Rosalind Kerven*

In her seaside Shetland home, Tess is torn between the plight of the whales and loyalty to her father and his job on the oil rig. A haunting and thought-provoking novel.

BACK HOME *Michelle Magorian*

A marvellously gripping story of an irrepressible girl's struggle to adjust to a new life. Twelve-year-old Rusty, who had been evacuated to the United States when she was seven, returns to the grey austerity of post-war Britain.

THE BEAST MASTER *Andre Norton*

Spine-chilling science fiction — treachery and revenge! Hosteen Storm is a man with a mission to find and punish Brad Quade, the man who killed his father long ago on Terra, the planet where life no longer exists.